A FAMILY SEEKS SECURITY *in the* DEEP WOODS

FOOTPRINTS
Under the
PINES

I0524793

DAWN BATTERBEE MILLER

DocUmeant *Publishing*

244 5th Avenue
Suite G-200
NY, NY 10001
646-233-4366

www.DocUmeantPublishing.com

DocUmeant Publishing 85 N. Main Street, Florida, NY 10921, 646-233-4366 (a division of DocUmeant) functions only as book publisher. As such, the ultimate design, content, editorial accuracy, and views expressed or implied in this work are those of the author.

Unless otherwise noted, all Scriptures are taken from the Holy Bible, New International Version®, NIV®. Copyright © 1973, 1978, 1984 by the International Bible Society. Used by permission of Zondervan. All rights reserved.

Scripture references marked KJV are taken from the King James Version of the Bible.

Scripture references marked NASB are taken from the New American Standard Bible, © 1960, 1963, 1968, 1971, 1972, 1973, 1975, 1977 by The Lockman Foundation. Used by permission.

Ginger Marks
DocUmeant Designs
Design & Layout

www.DocUmeantDesigns.com

ISBN 13: 978-1-937801-41-0
ISBN 10: 1-937801-41-1

Library of Congress Catalog Card Number: 2007902430

DEDICATION

I would like to say thank you to my friends and family who were willing to share their midwest pioneering experiences and to those who were so very patient when I seemed to steer most conversations to discussions of logging territory and the deep woods.

But most of all I want to express my deepest gratitude to my dear husband who was always there to listen and to comment as I read excerpts from the developing story and to urge me forward in my aspirations.

PROLOGUE

Seven year old Katherine Baines sat in her compartment on the S.S. Winslow with tears trickling down her cheeks. Fear rippled in her gut, threatening to spill her lunch onto the floor. She opened her suitcase and retrieved the pictures that were prepared before her mama's death in Sussex, England. A tear splashed onto her mother's face, creating a permanent stain.

The door opened and the steward appeared. "Come with me," he said. "We're about to dock in Canada."

Katherine stuffed the pictures into her case and followed the man to the main deck. "There," the man said, pointing, "that woman will watch over you while you're en route."

Katherine stepped through the gate and reached for the woman's hand, but the woman claimed Katherine's suitcase instead, leading the young girl onto the train and depositing her to await arrival in Bounding, Ontario. "Ma'am?" Katherine's voice trembled in her throat. "Will it be a long time?"

"It'll be a while, but you'll be okay. I'll be right here." The woman patted Katherine's shoulder and then walked away.

Several hours later Katherine met her Aunt Margaret, a tall thin lady with graying hair, whom she'd never seen and who would now be her mother.

Katherine stayed with her Aunt Margaret over the next five years, and though the woman was not a loving caregiver, neither was she unkind, and Katherine learned to care deeply for this woman who had taken her in.

Then Aunt Margaret returned to England, leaving twelve-year-old Katherine in the care of a local widow.

Tossed from one home to another, Katherine learned to adapt to her surroundings.

Then came that wonderful day when Katherine married Frank McLean to become his wife and the mother of his two adolescent children. It seemed that security was at last within her grasp. How could she have known that this relationship would lead her deep into the untamed forest and the rough and rowdy world of the late nineteenth-century lumberjack?

CHAPTER ONE

Blistering, red flames gobbled at the walls and ceilings of the only real home Katherine McLean had known since early childhood. Smoke billowed from windows; supporting timbers cracked and heaved; neighborhood volunteers pounded at the flames with blankets and shovels.

"Haul the fire pump over here," someone shouted. "Wet down the doorway so Clay can get out."

"Too late," another hollered. "Pump's out of water."

"Well, go open the cistern."

"We can't; the lid's rusted down."

Katherine peered through the haze, breathing with sandpaper breath. Where was Clay? What was keeping him? Why didn't he come out of that inferno with her son?

A shadow swirled in the smoke-filled doorway, and a hush washed over the milling crowd. Was it Clay? Did he have Johnny—or was it a mirage, a figment of Katherine's desperation? The vapor churned, and Katherine held her breath.

Suddenly, a figure burst into the light.

"My baby!" Katherine screamed. "He's got my baby."

She darted into a shower of sparks and burning debris. "My baby! Give me my baby."

"Get her out of here," Clay snapped.

A fireman took Katherine's arm. "Mrs. McLean, you need to stay back. We'll take care of the baby."

"No, he's my baby. Give me my baby."

Katherine wrenched free and lunged for Johnny. Then, familiar arms closed about her shoulders.

"C'mon, Katie, we need to get back."

"No, Frank, I want my baby." Katherine struggled in combat with her husband's iron grip.

"You couldn't help, Katie. You'd only be in the way."

Frank held Katherine close, until the fight drained from her body. She fell onto his chest, weeping.

Just then the crowd broke and a tall, thin man about thirty years old emerged, walking straight toward the fireman and Katherine's baby boy. His dark hair lay across his forehead, and his suit coat hung open. He carried a black bag.

"Doctor Rogers, Doctor Rogers!"

Helen Clemens, Katherine's neighbor, burst from the crowd, pointing at her white clapboard house across the street. Clay and the doctor moved toward it, and the throng parted for their passing, closing like a flood in their wake. Katherine and Frank elbowed their way in strong pursuit.

"Doctor Rogers is in the bedroom with Johnny," Helen said as she opened the door to them. "He'd like you to wait in the parlor."

Katherine's impatience erupted. "Why can't I see my baby? I want my baby."

Frank slipped his arm around her shoulders and pulled her close. "It's all right, Katie," he said. "The doctor needs time to do his job."

Katherine slumped against her husband's chest. "Thank you, Helen."

Frank guided Katherine into the sitting room where they sat waiting, trembling with fear.

Soon Katherine's longtime friend and neighbor, Sally Morris, entered the room. With her came Katherine's two teenaged stepchildren, Seth and Hannah, and her four-year-old daughter, Faith Ann, conceived out of wedlock before Katherine was eighteen. The family waited in silence.

"Pa," Faith Ann said at last, "where's Johnny? They took our baby, and they didn't give him back."

"Johnny's in the other room," Frank whispered. "The doctor is taking care of him."

"Well, he's ours. They can't have him."

"You're right." Frank held Faith Ann close, and she leaned against his chest.

Finally . . . a lifetime later, the doctor entered the room. He didn't need to speak; his face told the story.

"Johnny's gone. He died in his sleep . . . of asphyxiation."

Johnny's gone—asphyxiation. The words echoed in Katherine's psyche. Her world stood suspended in empty space.

"Would you like to see the boy?"

Frank took Katherine's arm and they moved toward the bedroom.

Katherine stumbled toward the place where Johnny lay and stood in silence, staring at her baby's lifeless form, the only child of her marriage to Frank. He was so beautiful, lying there with his arms folded across his chest, and his eyes closed as if in sleep. She leaned into Frank and he into her, mingling their tears in a pool of pain.

An eternity passed, and the ache in Katherine's heart lingered. She brushed her hand over Johnny's torso, and a floodgate of pain opened. Then she collapsed into anguished sobbing, weeping until she could cry no more.

Finally Frank spoke. "C'mon Katie, we need to get back to the kids."

Katherine's body followed her husband out of the room, but her heart remained, hovering over Johnny's lifeless form.

In the living room, Dr. Rogers stood with the family. "Do you folks have a place to sleep tonight?"

Katherine could only nod, as Frank spoke. "Sally has invited us to stay with her for a while."

"Then you probably should get on over there. The firemen'll take care of things here, and your kids need to get away from all this commotion."

Frank turned. "He's right; we need to go."

Faith Ann's brown eyes grew into pools of concern. "Ain't Johnny coming? We gotta get Johnny."

Katherine knelt and hugged her little girl, exhibiting a bravery she did not feel. "Johnny can't come, sweetheart. He's gone to be with Jesus." Katherine said the words, but her heart resisted their impact.

"Well, Jesus can have him for today, but we want him back tomorrow."

Katherine grasped her little girl's hand and followed Frank along Hilltop Ridge toward Sally Morris's home. As she walked, she looked down the slope at Lake Huron . . . so near and yet so far. All the water in that giant reservoir had been unable to prevent the flames from shattering Katherine's life.

All that evening the atmosphere in Mama Sally's house felt like a morgue. Supper was served with little conversation and little food consumed. Katherine and Sally arranged sleeping quarters for the family, communicating in an emotionless monotone. Frank sat silent and motionless, his face a portrait of desolation. Seth and Hannah murmured an empty goodnight and wandered off to their rooms. Faith Ann was tucked into bed with a kiss.

Drenched in pain, Katherine wandered upstairs to her room—to the room she'd used after Aunt Margaret left her at age twelve. The lace curtains Mama Sally had made still draped the windows, with the chest of drawers along the south wall. Katherine's writing table stood in the corner, and the old iron bed still sagged in the middle. Katherine collapsed onto it, fully dressed, and descended into a deep, fitful sleep.

The next morning, Katherine awoke, momentarily confused and disoriented. She reached for Frank, but his place on the bed was empty. She lay for several minutes suspended between night and day.

Then the tragedy of her loss filtered in. Grief flooded her being, and her heart groaned in agony. She rose and went outside, where the morning air nipped at her nose and cheeks, a perfect match for the icy tourniquet that squeezed her chest.

Katherine walked without purpose, drowning in the void that filled her soul. She remembered the emptiness she'd felt at age seven when her parents died of consumption. She remembered her fear when they sent her off to Canada to live with Aunt Margaret.

And she remembered her joy when she married Frank and gained the security of a real home. But now it was gone, whisked away in a moment's time.

Pain and anger mingled in Katherine's breast—pain for her loss and anger at a God who seemed to strike at her with every forward step. Who was this God, this God who hated her so much?

Katherine wandered aimlessly, until she found herself standing on Hilltop Ridge, gazing at the burned-out ruins of her home. A cold wind whistled up the hill from Lake Huron, lashing at her clothing and whipping her uncombed hair. What did it matter if she looked a mess? Her world was an abyss that threatened to suck her into its bowels. She lifted her eyes to the flame-blackened half-walls that stood as ugly reflections of death. She choked on the stench of wet ash, and nausea roiled in her stomach. From somewhere in the vastness of space she could hear a baby's soft cry. The baby wanted his mama.

Eventually, a crunching sound in the gravel told Katherine that someone was approaching. Frank came close, put his arm around her, and laid his cheek against her hair.

"Katie, are you all right?"

"Oh, Frank," Katherine cried. "It's happened again. My life has been torn apart." She buried her face against his chest and let the tears flow.

"It's OK, Katie." Frank pulled her close. "Johnny didn't feel any pain. He was just carried into heaven as he slept."

Katherine leaned into Frank, drawing strength from his assurance.

"We still have each other," he whispered, "and Seth and Hannah and Faith Ann. We'll hold Johnny in our hearts and rebuild our lives. We'll be a happy family."

After a few moments, Frank drew back and Katherine lifted her face, looking into his eyes that were calling out their love. This was the man she married—a man she could trust.

"We need to go back, Katie," he said. "They'll be looking for us."

Katherine walked with her husband along the hilltop toward Sally Morris' home. As they neared the house, Seth came out to meet them. His gangly arms hung at his sides, extending several inches below the sleeves of his green plaid shirt.

"How could this happen, Pa?" he asked. "Isn't it bad enough that Ma died? Why did Johnny have to die, too?"

Frank put his arm around the young man's shoulders. "I don't know, son. Sometimes life just takes these turns."

Katherine winced. *Life just takes these turns. Well, why is it always my life that takes these turns? Why can't God just leave me alone?*

But she said nothing. She trudged along beside her husband and stepson, and finally they entered Mama Sally's house. There they found thirteen-year-old Hannah standing by the cabinet, washing dishes. Her lithe young figure was draped in one of Grandma Sally's blue gingham aprons, and her honey-colored hair hung in a long braid down her back.

Four-year-old Faith Ann, now Katherine's only natural child, stood on a stool beside her stepsister with a spoon and a dishtowel in her hand.

"Well, Faith Ann, I see you're helping Hannah with the dishes," Katherine said. "What a good girl you are."

Hannah's face grew tight. She turned and slammed a pot into the dishpan. Water splashed all over the cupboard and ran across the counter, nearly dribbling onto the floor.

A ridge of frustration slithered up Katherine's spine. Why did Hannah have to be so unmanageable? Wasn't it enough that Johnny was gone? You'd think she'd be weeping with the rest of the family instead of slamming things all over the place. Katherine wanted to scream. She wanted to cry. She wanted to shake Hannah until the girl realized what she was doing to herself and her family.

"Mama," Faith Ann said, "Grandma Sally says Johnny's up in heaven, and we can go there to see him someday. Is that right?"

A flood of pain devoured the frustration, and Katherine nearly fell back, weeping. "Yes, I guess that's right," she managed to say.

She reached for her baby girl and then withdrew, her heart felt too wrenched for further discussion. She would talk to Faith Ann later.

Katherine entered the parlor and lowered herself into Mama Sally's high-backed wooden rocker. She looked out the window at the community church, with its steeple standing above the trees. She and Frank had taken Johnny to that church for ceremonial blessings soon after he was born, slightly over a year ago. Tomorrow their baby boy would lie before the altar, the preacher would say a prayer, and Johnny would be gone forever.

The rocking chair made a creaking, almost hypnotic sound against the cold, wooden floor. *Johnny's gone, Johnny's gone, Johnny's gone,* it seemed to say.

CHAPTER TWO

Hannah stood near the kitchen door of Grandma Sally's home. A big, wood-burning range stood along one wall, and the smell of baking bread, set to rise the night before, filled the air. A table with a washbowl and pitcher stood beside it. Near the door, the family's coats hung on a row of nails.

"Pa, can Faith Ann go with me to Mrs. Petrie's house today?"

"Hannah, you know better. Katherine needs Faith Ann here."

Faith Ann's lip trembled, and Hannah could feel her sister's disappointment.

"But I want to go with Hannah."

"Faith Ann, you can't go. Your mother needs you."

"But, Mrs. Petrie tells such good stories. I'll be a good girl. I won't be a bother."

Hannah gritted her teeth, waiting for the answer she knew was coming.

"It's not a question of whether you'll be a good girl. I know you'll be a good girl, but your mama needs you. She misses Johnny, and you can help her feel better."

Out of the corner of her eye, Hannah saw Katherine lurking in the dining room. How dare she stand there shuffling through drawers as if she were looking for something? Hannah knew better. Her stepmother was listening in. Well, she was going to get an earful this time.

Hannah raised her voice just enough to be sure Katherine could hear. "Katherine's just a selfish old busybody with no concern for anyone but herself."

A smile of satisfaction curled Hannah's lips, as Katherine's chin dropped onto her chest. That woman deserved just what she got.

"Hannah, that's enough! If you say one more word . . ." Pa pointed a finger and Hannah clamped her jaw shut. "Seth and I are going to Grandpa McLean's house to build a box stall for Gretchen to foal. You are going to Mrs. Petrie's house alone. And Faith Ann is staying here with her mother."

Hannah snatched her jacket from a nail and went outside, careful not to slam the door lest her father become more upset than he was already. She threw her jacket over her shoulders, muttering to herself.

"Who does Katherine think she is? Does she think she's the only one in the family who hurts because Johnny died? All she ever thinks about is herself. Why did Pa go and marry her in the first place? We were happy the way we were. We didn't need a selfish, interfering old woman around."

Hannah thought about her own mother and all the weeks and months she had suffered before she died. Hannah could remember the crackles that echoed in her ma's chest throughout that long winter. Although Hannah had been only seven at the time, she could still remember the day her mother called her to the bedside.

"Baby," her ma had said, "I'm going away for a long time. Don't be sad for me. Just be a good girl, mind your pa, and I'll see you in heaven some day."

Hannah sighed. Heaven was a long way off. In the meantime, she had to live with Katherine.

But today was Saturday, and good things were in store. At the end of the day, Velma Petrie would give her five cents for keeping old Mrs. Petrie company while Velma went to the village. If Hannah added the nickel to her savings, she'd have enough money to get her initials engraved on Great-grandmother Hamlin's brooch. She smiled as she thought of the day Grandma McLean had given the brooch to her. "Great Grandma Hamlin would want you to have it," she'd said.

Hannah's heart swelled with emotion. She pulled the heirloom from her pocket, carefully removed it from the velvet bag it had come in, and fingered the black opal. She brushed the golden whorls that held it fast, scanning its back for Grandmother Hamlin's initials. After today, the casing would read H.M.H. for Hannah May Hamlin, and right below, it would read H.E.M. for Hannah Elizabeth McLean.

"Hey Hannah."

Hannah jumped. "Millie Wilkins, what are you hollerin' about? You nearly scared the wits out of me." She squeezed her inheritance tightly, savoring the familial bond it represented.

Hannah's friend raced to the road. "Hannah, you'll never guess what happened." She leaned close, speaking in a conspiratorial hush.

"I don't have any idea. What happened?"

"C'mon, guess."

Hannah had no interest in Millie's little game, but she threw out an idea, hoping it would appease her friend.

"Your pa is taking you shopping in the city."

"Nope." Millie shook her head and flashed a gleeful smile.

"You got a job at McGregors'."

"Nope."

"Oh c'mon, Millie, what happened?"

"Horace Collins is coming over to help me with my arithmetic."

"Horace Collins! Oh, Millie, how did you ever manage that?"

"Well, after I got my test back yesterday, I was hollerin' that I was gonna flunk and all . . . and, well . . . Horace just walked up and said, 'If you want, I could come over and help you study.'"

Millie's eyes widened, and her face grew intense. "If I want him to come over and help me study! Do I want a hundred dollars? I just about fainted."

"Oh, Millie, that's so exciting! Maybe he's going to ask you to the harvest festival next week."

"If he does, I'll die. I'll just die!"

"Well, don't die before I tell you about my brooch."

Hannah opened her hand, revealing the pin. "Just look what I got for my birthday last night." She held out the heirloom for Millie to see. "It belonged to my Great-grandmother Hamlin. Her birthday was in October, like mine, and I got her same name. So that's why I got the brooch. The black opal is our birthstone."

Millie reached for the pin, brushing her fingers over the gold setting. She held it up, and it sparkled in the sun.

"It's an heirloom," Hannah explained, "and when my kids and grandkids come along, I'll pass it down to them. I'm going to get my initials engraved on the back, right here with hers, see?"

The girls babbled excitedly until Hannah noticed Gordy Bixby across the street. Nearly six feet tall, with dark hair and eyes, he was the most handsome thing Hannah had ever seen.

She smiled and waved. "Hi, Gordy."

But Gordy didn't even pause. He simply returned the greeting and went on down the street.

Hannah sighed. "I'd give just about anything to go to the festival with him . . . but he never gives me a second thought."

"You know." Millie's eyes danced in covert disclosure as she spoke. "The old Butcher farm right down the road from him is for sale now. My pa was talking about it just this morning. Wouldn't it be grand if your pa bought it? Then Gordy'd have to notice you, because you'd be neighbors."

"With my luck, he'd treat me like I was his little sister."

Just then, Millie's front door opened, and her ma appeared in the doorway.

"Millie, you get in here right now and finish these dishes."

"I'm coming, Ma."

Millie dawdled for a minute, chattering about the coming festival and the chances of winning a date with Horace Collins, until her mother reappeared.

"Millie, you get in here . . . this instant."

"Look, Hannah, I have to go, but I'll see you in church Sunday."

Millie ran inside, shouting her goodbyes as she went.

Hannah returned her heirloom to its black velvet bag and pulled the drawstring tight. She put it in her pocket and headed north toward Velma Petrie's house.

Katherine sat in her rocker, mending Seth's flannel shirt. Faith Ann sat on the floor nearby, playing with her white sock doll, Annie. The little girl lifted the doll and looked deep into her black, shirt-button eyes.

"Annie, you can have some breakfast after your face is washed."

Annie stared back at Faith Ann out of lifeless eyes and said nothing.

Faith Ann brushed her hand over Annie's face, picked up an imaginary spoon, and lifted it to the line of red stitches that represented Annie's mouth. After feeding her doll several bites of imaginary oatmeal, Faith Ann put the imaginary spoon back onto the floor. She smoothed the folds of Annie's pink flowered dress.

"All right, now that you've finished your breakfast, you may go out to play."

Laying her dolly aside, Faith Ann climbed onto her mother's lap.

"Mama," she said, "why did God give Johnny to us, if he was just going to take him back again?"

"I don't know, sweetheart." Tears brimmed in Katherine's eyes. "Some things just happen." She pulled her baby close. "Here, let me tell you a story."

Faith Ann leaned against her mother's chest, and Katherine began to rock.

"A long time ago, in a far away land called England, your mama lived in a nice little house with her mama and her daddy. Then one day my parents got very sick and went away to heaven. After that, I came to Canada to live with my Aunt Margaret. I was a little girl then, just a little older than you are now. Everything here in Canada was so different from my home in England that I was afraid to do much of anything. Finally, I grew up and married your pa. Soon after that, a little baby girl was born. That baby girl was you, Faith Ann. And you made me very happy."

"Did Johnny make you happy?"

"Oh, yes. When Johnny came along, I thought nothing could ever make me sad again. I had two babies, a boy and a girl. And I loved you both very much."

"But Johnny died, and you got sad."

"Yes, sweetheart. But I still have you, and you still make me happy."

"Why do you cry then, if I make you happy?"

"I cry when I think that you won't have a baby brother to play with."

"Don't worry about me, Mama. I'll be OK."

Faith Ann patted her mother's arm. "You can smile and be happy, because I can play with Annie."

She slid onto the floor and reached for the doll. "See, Mama, we can be a family, and you don't need to cry."

Katherine looked down at her baby girl, so innocent and yet so brave. Her stomach knotted into a ball of shame. Katherine had been depending on that little girl's strength to bolster her own fortitude. Her heart sickened at the thought of her own weakness. How could she have been so selfish? She reached for her sewing basket and jammed the needle through the shirtsleeve, pulling the thread tight. Then and there she determined to look toward the future instead of crying over the past.

Minutes later, the kitchen door opened.

"Faith Ann." It was Hannah arriving home from the Petries'. "Faith Ann, c'mere. I brought you something."

Faith Ann tossed Annie aside and ran out of the room.

"Cookies," the little girl shouted from the kitchen. "You brought me cookies! Mama, Hannah brought me cookies."

Katherine smiled at the friendship between Faith Ann and Hannah. She only wished she could relate as well with her stepdaughter. If anyone in this world could appreciate the emptiness in Hannah's heart, it surely was Katherine. She had lived in that incredible, lonely place that comes when you've been thrown into a hostile world without a mother. There must be a way to reach Hannah. There must be a way, if only she could figure out what it was.

CHAPTER THREE

Frank tossed a seventy-five-pound bag of cracked corn onto a wagon at Fritz's Seed 'n' Feed. Standing erect, he rested his hands on his aching back. Twenty bags to go—nineteen, eighteen, seventeen, sixteen. Leaning into the job, he swung the bags in rhythm.

Fifteen, fourteen, thirteen. His muscles screamed for relief as he tossed one bag after another. Five, four, three, two, one.

He took a deep breath and stood erect, brushing the dust and chaff from his pants and shirt. He wiped his hands one against the other to remove the dirty residue and then walked toward the merchandising area of the store.

"Got 'em loaded, Fritz," he called.

"Thanks, Frank."

Opening the cash drawer, Fritz pulled out three quarters and handed them to Frank.

"Thanks again for the help, and if you don't find a job before next week, c'mon back."

"I appreciate that, Fritz."

Frank's voice spoke the words, but the overworked muscles in his back shouted their opposition. Almost any job he could think of looked better than stacking feed all morning next Saturday.

He stuffed the money into his pocket and left the store, fingering the letter that lay there. It had arrived in the morning mail a few days earlier, and he'd read it a dozen times.

Dear Frank,

I received a letter from your pa the other day. He says you lost everything in a house fire, and even the shoe shop was completely destroyed. I'm really sorry to hear that. He says you've been looking for work all over Bounding and there's none to be had, so I thought you should know there's plenty of work here in northern Michigan.

I know it's hard to leave the home you've known all your life, but if you're looking for work and a place to live, Michigan might be the answer.

Logging is still strong here, and the busy season is about to begin. Your cousin Jasper is teaming up with the Luc DuBois camp this winter, and he says they're looking for a clerk. With your background running the shoe shop, it seems like a good job for you.

As for housing, there's an abandoned house here in Hitchcock that you could get for back taxes. It's an old fieldstone house, and I hear most of the furniture is still there. When the owner died a couple years back, his widow left it all and went to Grand Rapids to live with her folks.

Let me know if you're coming, and I'll meet you at the tracks.

Uncle Ned

The idea of leaving Bounding and running off to Michigan sent a bullet through Frank's chest. Michigan might as well be a million miles away. He'd never see his folks again, and he wouldn't be there when they grew too old to work the farm. His folks had always been willing to help when he needed them, and should he now run off and leave them?

They'd been there when his first wife, Susanna, contracted consumption.

"Why don't you just move out here with us?" his folks had said.

So Frank moved into his parents' home with his sick wife and two rambunctious kids. His mother and father had watched over Suzanna, and even built a porch where she could sleep in the open air. They never voiced a complaint about the rasping cough that must have kept them awake night after night, and they'd watched the children after Susanna died.

How could Frank desert them now, as they were getting older? There must be another way.

He turned his steps northward toward Hal Benning's mill. Maybe Hal could use a hand. It was his last hope.

Nearing the edge of town, Frank could see the old mill with its unpainted gray shingles hanging askew. The pungent aroma of freshly cut pine filled the air, and the shrill whine of the saw assaulted his ears.

He drew near the building, and his heart throbbed with desperation. "Well, here goes nothing," he muttered.

He stepped inside to find Hal guiding a hefty log into the monster saw. Beyond the saw, a two-inch slab of wood dropped into a trough. One day that slab might become a rafter in someone's home, or maybe a floor joist or a stud, holding a wall in place.

"How's it goin', Hal?" Frank called.

Hal flipped a switch, and the saw ground to a halt. The big steam engine belched and huffed, but the wheel continued to turn, creating a constant hum.

"So what's up, Frank?"

Frank removed his cap, fingering its bill. "Actually, I was hoping you might be able to use a helper."

Hal brushed his wrist across his forehead to wipe away the sweat beads that clustered there.

"I wish I could, Frank, but I just can't afford to put on a man right now." His face reflected an honest desire to be of help to his friend. "Have you checked with Fritz? Someone said he needs a stock man."

A wave of hopelessness cascaded over Frank's shoulders. "I just came from there—stacked bags all morning. But Fritz doesn't need a full-time man, and I've got a family to support."

"I'm sorry, Frank, but I just can't do it."

Frank exited the building with his heart in his shoes. Behind him, the whine of the saw rose to a piercing scream.

Walking south along Main Street, Frank observed the seawall about a hundred feet out in Lake Huron. Without that wall, the waves would pluck away at the shore, snatching a pebble at a time until the entire beach was gone. Could a man's life be eroded away in similar manner? How long before Frank's vitality might be torn asunder by the ripping, tearing forces of time? Where might a man find materials to build a seawall that would protect himself and his family?

"Hello, Mr. Frank. How are ya?"

Frank looked up to see simple-minded Harvey Weaver coming down the street toward him. Harvey had been one of Frank's best customers before the shop burned. His bowed legs always wore the outside edges of his shoes until they looked— and must have felt—lopsided and miserable. Frank had put on heel plates a couple of times, but Harvey pulled them off. "They felt funny," he said, "and they made marks on my ma's varnished floors."

Frank's heart pinched; all that was in the past, for Frank had repaired his last shoe.

"I'm OK I guess, Harvey, and yourself?"

"I'm fine, Mr. Frank. 'Ceptin' I ain't got nobody to fix up my shoes no more. When're ya gonna start yer shop up agin? This town needs a good shoe man."

"All my equipment's gone, Harvey, and I can't afford to buy new."

"That's a bad thing, Mr. Frank. You was a good shoe man."

"Thanks, Harvey. I appreciate your confidence."

Frank visited with Harvey for several minutes before he lifted his cap, brushed his hand over his brown hair, and turned to go.

"See you later, Harvey. I gotta go now and pick up a newspaper to check for a job opening somewhere." He resettled his cap, pressing it firmly into place.

"OK, Mr. Frank. See ya later."

As Frank continued down Main Street, he considered his future. This was his town; he'd known it since he was a boy. To his left lay Lake Huron, and to his right stood a single row of stores that made up the shopping district. Northernmost was Fritz's Seed n' Feed, McGregors' General Store, and Ma Bailey's Bakery. To the south stood Dunwoody's Barber Shop and McCauley's Farm Supply with the post office and the fire station. Near the end of the village stood the church with the graveyard, where Johnny's body lay.

Frank's shoulders trembled at the thought of his baby boy lying in the cold, dark earth. He pinched back tears that threatened to spill down his cheeks, and turned westward up the hill.

Without realizing it, he quickened his steps. Maybe there'd be a job listing in the *County Herald*.

Within a few minutes, Frank stood in front of Eisenberg's Newsstand, examining the sign that hung on the door: *Closed: Be back after while, Hans.*

So what was new? Hans was probably down at the barbershop swapping stories with his buddies, or maybe at McGregors', shooting the breeze with old Mr. Popov. At any rate, the likelihood of a job listing was slim at best.

Continuing up the hill, Frank headed toward Barnes Avenue and his burned-out home. Why, he did not know.

He crested the hill, and the fire-blackened remains of his house came into view. He wandered around the north side, where his shop had been. Unmended shoes cluttered the ashes—half burned, soaked, and shrunken into grotesque shapes. Those were his neighbors' shoes. They had been entrusted to him for renewal.

It was then that his eyes fell upon one tiny, white shoe, size 00, disfigured and misshapen. His shoulders convulsed, and a sob broke from his chest.

"Frank, get hold of yourself," he said aloud.

But the tears broke loose and rolled down his cheeks. He stood for many long minutes, pinching back tears that oozed from his eyes and wiping his cheeks with his hands. Finally, he turned away and headed for the Morris home.

As he came within sight of Mama Sally's house, Hannah came running out to meet him. Her azure eyes, so like her mother's, sparkled, and a big smile filled her face.

"Pa, look! Mel Johnson put my initials on the back of Greatgrandma Hamlin's brooch. They're right beneath hers, see?"

Frank didn't feel much like celebrating, but he took the brooch, brushing his fingers over the back.

"Sure enough," he said. "There are your initials, right under Grandma Hamlin's." His face transformed into a smile he did not feel. "You'll want to take real good care of this. It's an heirloom."

"You're right, Pa. I'm going to keep it in my hope chest, and I'll never let it go."

Hannah's eyes glowed with intensity as she went on. "By the way, Pa, Millie says the old Coursey place is for sale. That'd be a good place to buy. It's a little out of town, but not that far. We could walk to town whenever we needed to."

The frustration of the morning came pouring forth, and Frank spat a response before he thought. "For Pete's sake, Hannah, think. I ain't got a job. Have you forgotten?"

Hannah winced and drew back. "I'm sorry, Pa, I . . ."

"Well, next time, think."

Hannah's face twisted in anguish. "I didn't mean no harm, Pa. I just . . ."

The hurt in Hannah's voice nipped at Frank's conscience, but he went on. "Another house is simply not something we can think about right now. We'll be lucky if I can earn enough money to feed this family. I've had a hard day, I'm hungry and exhausted, and I don't need any lip."

Hannah burst into tears and dashed into the other room.

Frank poured coffee from the pot on the back of the stove and slumped into a chair at the kitchen table. He selected a slice of bread, covered it with a thick layer of bacon grease, and sat, trying to ease the agony in his chest. Weariness in his body hung on him like a dead horse.

Frank sat for many minutes meditating on his situation. His family had no home. He had no job, no income, and no stability. Something had to be done, and it was his job to do it. Pulling Uncle Ned's letter from his pocket, he scanned it again.

If you're looking for work and a place to live, Michigan might be the answer. There's an abandoned house in Hitchcock that you could get for back taxes.

Frank dropped his head into his hands, rubbing his brow with his fingertips. He knew what he had to do, and it broke his heart.

Later that evening, Frank lay waiting for Katherine to join him in the old iron bed Mama Sally had made available to them. He watched as she unfastened the pins in her long, chestnut-colored hair. He observed the gentle ripple of the muscles in her arms as she pulled the comb through her tresses. She was a beautiful woman, and she was his. His heart reached out with love as Katherine leaned over the washbowl, patted her face with cold water, and dried it on the towel by the washstand.

"C'mon to bed, Katie. It's getting late."

"OK, I'm coming." Katherine cupped her hands over the lamp and blew into it, plunging the room into blackness. Finally the light of Frank's life lay beside him.

"Katie," he said, "I didn't find a job today."

"Something will turn up, Frank. I know it will, and you'll take good care of us." She breathed a long, sleepy sigh.

"There are no jobs available around here, Katie. We're going to have to make some difficult choices."

"Something will turn up. I know it will."

Frank waited several seconds before he went on. "I know where I can get a job—a good job that pays real well."

"Then why are you so depressed? Just go get it."

"The job is in northern Michigan."

"Northern Michigan! Surely you're not serious, Frank. What about the children? We can't go dragging them off to some untamed wilderness."

"They'll just have to get used to it."

"And what about your folks? Are you just going to run off and leave them?"

"Bert lives just thirty-five miles away. He's their son, too, and he could get here if they really needed him."

"And how are we going to get there—swim?"

"Don't forget, we still have the boat. *Miranda* was down at the dock and didn't burn with the house. We could take her across the lake, sell her in Port Huron, and use the money for train tickets to Hitchcock."

"You're going all the way across Lake Huron in a rowboat? Frank, think! It would never work. We can't just go wandering around Lake Huron in a rowboat."

"I know we could do it, Katherine. We'd cross at Blue Point. It's only fifteen miles to Michigan right there. It's Indian summer, and we'd have nice weather for the trip. When we get to Hitchcock, we can build a whole new life for ourselves."

"And where would we live when we get to Hitchcock? I don't want to move in with your Uncle Ned. I lived with a stranger when I was a kid . . . and I didn't like it."

"It wouldn't be for very long. Uncle Ned says there's a house in Hitchcock that we could get for back taxes. It's even got furniture in it."

"And where would we stay while we sell *Miranda*? We can't afford a hotel for five people."

"We'll row down the shore 'til we find somebody who'll put us up."

"Frank, that's the dumbest thing you've said yet. We're just going to walk up to some stranger's door and say, 'How about a room for the night, one for us and two more for our kids?"

"Yes. People are basically kind. Some may turn us down, but there'll be somebody willing to put us up. And if not, we'll pull *Miranda* onto the shore and sleep in her."

"Are you going to insist on this thing?"

"I don't know what else to do, Katie."

"Frank, I don't think I can stand this turmoil."

Katherine rolled over with her face to the wall.

Hours later, Frank lay awake thinking about a move to northern Michigan. The more he thought about it, the more it seemed the thing to do. He knew the idea scared Katherine nearly to death, but it was the only answer to their situation. As soon as he could, he'd buy a lathe and make canthooks and peavies for the lumber industry. Later, he'd make window frames and doorsills and mantels for fireplaces and things. He'd become well off, maybe even rich, and his family wouldn't want for a thing. Katherine would come around; she had to. There was no other way.

Chapter Four

Katherine sat on *Miranda*'s bench at the stern, looking out across Lake Huron. Faith Ann sat beside her holding Annie, and Hannah sat on a center bench with a small case that held Grandma Hamlin's brooch, a few pictures, and the things she'd taken from her hope chest. Some water and a sack lunch had been deposited beneath the stern seat. Everything else the family owned—a comb, a few washcloths, a bar of soap, a couple of towels, some underwear, and one clean outfit for each member of the family—had been stuffed into a pillowcase and stashed under the oarsman's bench, where Frank sat rowing. The day was hazy but warm, and the family had shed their coats, tossing them over the bench beside Hannah.

As the boat navigated through the water, Katherine's mind traveled back to the day Seth announced his decision to remain in Ontario.

"Pa," Seth had said, "I've decided not to go to Michigan. I'm going to stay and help Grandpa McLean run the farm."

Pain had overspread Frank's face. "Son," he said, "do you realize what you're saying? It's a long way to Michigan. Chances are you'll never see us again."

"I know, Pa." Seth's face grew serious. "But I'm almost sixteen now, and Grandpa needs me. I've been thinking about this for a while now, and I think it's the right thing to do."

Frank stood as if he'd been punched in the stomach. "You're sure this is what you want."

"I'm sure."

"You realize that once we're gone, there's no turning back."

"Yes, Pa. But it's the best thing for me and for Grandpa, too. I'll stay in Ontario to help with the work. Then one day the farm will be mine, and I can carry on for him. It's the way I want to spend my life."

"OK, if you're certain about this, I won't stand in your way. Just be very sure, that's all."

Frank had tossed in his sleep all that night, calling out to Seth and moaning about farming and emptiness and distance.

Faith Ann jerked on Katherine's sleeve. "Mama, Mama, are we there yet?"

"No, sweetheart, it'll be a long while before we get to Michigan."

"Hannah says there are wild animals in Michigan. Do you think I'll get to see a bear?"

A giant fist closed around Katherine's chest. She didn't want her little girl to see a bear, and she didn't want her chasing around in that wild forest. And she didn't want her accosted by some drunken lumberjack.

Katherine knew about Northern Michigan. It was nothing but a great big swamp, filled with trees and logging camps and lumberjacks who came to town to turn the place upside down with their drinking and carousing. It wasn't a place she wanted her family to be.

But Frank had said it was the only way, and she would support him in his decision.

Looking up, Katherine noticed Hannah staring over the water, her face a study in irritability. The girl had flown into a pout the day she learned of the move to Hitchcock. She grumbled constantly about leaving her friends and living in some wild, untamed wilderness. Well, Katherine didn't like it, either, but they were moving to Michigan, and Hannah might as well get used to the idea.

"Mama, I can't . . . ." Faith Ann jumped off the bench and lost her balance. Annie flipped into the water, trundling in *Miranda*'s wake.

"Mama, we gotta go back."

"No, Faith Ann," Hannah snapped. "We can't go back. Annie's gone and we'd never reach her."

"But I lost my doll!" Faith Ann's cries echoed over the water into oblivion.

"Sweetheart," Katherine said, "Annie's gone to dolly heaven."

Katherine drew her little one close, rocking back and forth in rhythm with the boat and thinking of Johnny. Faith Ann was suffering the pain of losing a loved one.

In time, both she and Faith Ann grew sleepy. "Hannah, will you spread the coats on the floor?" Katherine asked.

Hannah smoothed the coats into a pad, and Katherine lowered Faith Ann onto them. Finding herself on the floor, she leaned over the bench with her head in her arms. Soon both Katherine and Faith Ann were transported into semi-consciousness.

Like two peas in a pod, Hannah thought. *Faith Ann has Katherine. Katherine has my pa. My pa has Katherine and Faith Ann. And I have no one.* Tears filled Hannah's eyes. *I don't even have my friends anymore.* She thought about Bounding; she thought about Millie and Gordy Bixby and Horace Collins. Even Seth was gone. Why couldn't she have stayed in Bounding with Seth? Hannah gulped and took a deep breath. She bit her lip, holding back a sob.

Frank sat on the oarsman's bench, rowing. Dip and pull, dip and pull. He flexed his shoulders to relieve the tension in his back. Behind him only Hannah was alert.

"Keep your eyes peeled," he said. "We should be fairly near the coast by now."

Hannah lifted her hand to her brow, peering into the distance, while Frank continued to row. It had been a long, hard day, and Frank was ready for a break.

"I see it, Pa." Hannah leaned forward, pointing west. "I see land."

Excitement rippled in Frank's gut. Once his family was in Michigan, they'd sell *Miranda* and take the train to Hitchcock. He'd get a job in the camps, buy that fine stone house, and start a new life. He gripped the oars and pulled hard.

As *Miranda* neared the strand, a forest of tall pines appeared, reaching into the sky like giant fingers trying to grasp a cloud. A ridge of rocks lay along the shore with the swell of Lake Huron lapping endlessly against them. The panorama stretched as far as the eye could see—a majestic reception to a mighty land. Frank turned *Miranda* southward, where a gentle flow toward the St. Clair River carried the craft along.

Peering into the forest for some sign of life, Frank's attention was drawn to something moving in the underbrush.

"Hey look," he said. "A big buck . . . over there in the bushes . . . see it?"

Hannah leaned forward. "Yes, there he is. And there's a doe just off to the right, see?"

Frank scrutinized the area. "Sure enough, there she is."

Together, Frank and Hannah marveled at the majesty of nature and the grace God had granted His creatures. It was one of those moments, so rare these days, when Frank felt close to his daughter. He worried about Hannah. She had distanced herself when he married Katherine, and the rift seemed to have grown worse since she learned about the move to Michigan. But Hannah would learn to love her new home. She'd find new friends, and she'd be happy in Hitchcock. She had to; there was no other way.

"Now keep your eyes peeled for a place to spend the night," Frank called.

Katherine and Faith Ann awoke.

"Pa, are we in Michigan?" Faith Ann's eyes scanned her surroundings.

"Sure enough, that's Michigan," Frank responded and pulled on the oars.

As daylight gave way to dusk, and no refuge came in sight, Frank's nerves grew raw with agitation.

"Please God," he whispered, "we need a place to sleep."

Suddenly Hannah moved close. "Pa, look, a building. Maybe we could spend the night there."

Frank peered into the brush and cringed. A tarpaper shack was not the sort of place he had in mind, but it would provide a roof over their heads. He turned toward shore.

Almost before *Miranda* reached the sand, Hannah leaped overboard. "C'mon, let's see what's here."

"Now, wait a minute," Frank called. "We need to get this boat secured before you go running off."

He stepped overboard and boosted a sleepy-eyed Faith Ann into Hannah's arms. Then he reached for Katherine as she climbed ashore.

The building wasn't much. Most of the windows had been boarded up, and the eaves were rotted and broken. A large hasp that had once secured the door was torn loose. The door hung open.

Inside, the moon shining through the windows revealed a rough counter along one wall, and a kerosene lantern sat on one end. Frank lit the lantern, and the darkness receded.

A table and two chairs sat in the middle of the room, and by the east wall stood an old wooden box-bed with a lumpy straw tick on top. Hannah put Faith Ann onto it, and the little girl settled into almost instant slumber.

Frank tossed some kindling into the fireplace and set it ablaze. "Let's get some heat in here," he said. He added several larger pieces of wood and soon the fire burned brightly.

As warmth permeated the room, Hannah crawled onto the bed beside Faith Ann, fully dressed and wearing her coat. Within moments both girls slept soundly.

Katherine sat with her husband in the old shack in the woods.

Frank's elbows rested on the table and his head drooped over his hands. His shoulders shook as if in pain.

"Are you OK, Frank?"

He looked up with anguished eyes. "It's just . . . well . . . I was thinking about the way things were before and the way they are now. When I asked you to marry me, I promised to take care of you. Now here we are in this ungodly place, not knowing where our next meal is coming from or where we'll sleep tomorrow night. It's like everything has spun out of control."

"You aren't to blame for that fire, Frank. And the fire is what put us here. We found a nice, warm place for tonight, and tomorrow we'll be on our way."

Katherine smiled, trying to give encouragement. "We'll build a new life when we get to Hitchcock. We'll be all right."

Frank slapped the table with his palm. "This is not a nice, warm place. This is an abandoned old shack. It doesn't even have enough beds for us all."

"We're a strong, healthy family, Frank. We have each other, and we'll face our problems together. We'll overcome whatever obstacles we meet."

Tears welled in Frank's eyes, and he caressed Katherine's arm. "What would I do without you?" he whispered. "You are the joy of my life."

Katherine nestled in his embrace for several long minutes before she spoke. "We're going to beat all the odds," she whispered. "Now, c'mon, let's call it a day."

He banked the fire while she turned down the lantern's wick, and they retired for the night. Hannah and Faith Ann lay at one end of the bed, and Katherine and Frank lay at the other. In almost no time, the entire McLean family was asleep.

Katherine awoke the next morning to find the sunlight pressing through the dust-covered window over the bed. She rose and went outside, reveling in the crisp October morning.

Birds twittered in the trees, and Lake Huron lapped gently onto the Michigan shore.

Not far distant, Katherine found a rippling stream tumbling over a rocky creek bed. When her family was ready to leave, they'd fill the jug from this stream. There would be plenty of fresh water to drink while they traveled south. Katherine stood by the stream for several long minutes looking out at the strand and thinking of her family's trip across Lake Huron. Thoughts of Bounding and of Johnny and Seth filtered into her consciousness, and her heart wrenched with pain. She knelt and dabbled her fingers in the water, allowing its refreshing ambiance to soothe the emptiness in her heart. Then she pushed the discomfort to the back of her mind and headed back toward the building.

It was then she noticed a gnarled old tree with apples hanging from its branches. The fruit was scarred and misshapen, but with a little cleaning and coring they would provide a fine a snack for her family. She'd send the girls out to gather some of them after breakfast.

As she stepped inside, she found Frank and the girls up and about. A fire burned in the fireplace, and Hannah and Faith Ann huddled close to it. The lunch sack had been opened, and food was spread on the table.

"There's an old apple tree outside," she said, "and I thought the girls could pick some after we eat. I'll clean and core them for a snack on the way to Port Huron today."

"I'll get apples," Faith Ann sang. "I'm a big girl."

Katherine smiled at the precocious little girl's comment. "C'mon, everybody, let's eat."

The family dined on boiled eggs and bread-and-butter sandwiches. Katherine and Frank sat on the two chairs. Hannah sat on the bed, and Faith Ann ran back and forth between them.

After breakfast the girls collected a bundle of apples, and then Katherine peeled, cored, and dewormed them for lunch. Hannah filled the water jug from the stream, Frank put out the fire, and the family loaded *Miranda* for the trip to town.

CHAPTER FIVE

Frank plied the waters of Lake Huron, moving his family ever southward toward the big city. He thought about Seth, living on the old homestead with his grandparents, and he realized he would never see his son again. Was the young man OK? Was the farm doing well? Tears welled behind his eyes, as he thought of a tiny grave beside the church. Was it well cared for? Frank would never know. But that was behind him; he must look to the future and a new home for his family. He pulled hard on the oars.

Late that afternoon, Frank caught sight of the pier at Port Huron. He turned *Miranda* shoreward and guided her into a slip.

"Land ho!" he called. He could almost hear a sigh of relief from the boat behind him.

After the family climbed overboard and stretched their legs, they made their way along the dock toward the marina.

"Look at the boats," Hannah cried. "Have you ever seen so many different kinds?"

"I think they're having a party," Faith Ann offered.

Frank scanned the wharf. There were canoes and kayaks and sculls. There were flat-bottomed boats and houseboats and sailboats, most of them decked out as if for a special event.

"Good afternoon," the attendant said. "What can I do for you?"

"I'm Frank McLean, and this is my family." Frank reached out his hand. "My boat is down at the dock, and I need to sell her. We'd like to rent a space here for a while."

"Sure thing, we have a boat show scheduled next week, and you can probably sell her then."

Frank could hardly believe his good fortune. "Sounds like a perfect setup, Mr... . what did you say your name was?"

"Name's Doyle Winston, and the show runs from nine to four-thirty on Friday and Saturday."

"I'll be here," Frank said.

"Let me get the agreement forms for you."

Doyle Winston moved behind the counter and handed some papers to Katherine.

"One more thing," Frank said. "We need a place to stay 'til after the sale. I don't have much money, so it needs to be as cheap as possible. Got any ideas?"

The attendant stepped back, regarding Frank and his family with a slow, appraising once-over. "Well . . ." Doyle Winston peered at Frank over the tops of his glasses. "My folks live out north of town on Old Plank Road. They have rooms upstairs, and they'd probably be willing for you stay there for a few days. I'm sure it wouldn't cost much."

"Then, too, if you're able, you could help me get ready for the sale. I'll pick you up every morning and pay you seventy-five cents a day for the work."

Frank fell back, amazed at his good fortune. "When do I start?"

"How about tomorrow?" Doyle Winston stuffed the agreement papers in a file. "My folks place is five miles north of town. I'll take you there after closing, if you want to wait."

Frank and his family walked around the marina until five o'clock, when Doyle brought the buggy out front for them.

Thirty minutes later, Doyle reined in the horses at an old, two story farmhouse with weathered siding and missing shutters. A portly older gentleman stepped outside with shoulders back and thumbs tucked into his pockets.

"Pa, these are the McLeans," Doyle said. "They came across the lake from Blue Point, Ontario, and they need lodging for a few days."

The old man smiled but stood silent.

"Frank here has agreed to help with the boat show, and I told him you'd be willing to let them stay here until after the sale."

The man reached out a welcoming hand. "Glad to make your acquaintance, Mr. McLean. I'm Paul Winston, Doyle's pa. And if Doyle says you're OK, then you're OK with me."

Just then a petite, middle-aged woman, with sparkling eyes and tightly curled strawberry-gray hair, came through the doorway. "What's going on out here, Paul?"

Paul laid his arm across her shoulders in a good-natured, proprietary gesture. "Mandy, this here's the McLeans. I guess Frank's going to help Doyle with the boat show next week, and they need a place to stay."

"Well, this here's the place. Have you had your supper?"

"Not really," Doyle said. "They've been waiting around in the store since about four o'clock." He adjusted his cap and turned away. "See you later, Pa. And Frank, I'll be by for you about five o'clock in the morning."

Mandy Winston turned toward the house. "Paul, why don't you take Frank and the girls out to see that new colt," she said, "while we women get supper?"

"Good idea." Paul Winston looked down at Faith Ann. "Guess what? We got a brand new baby horse."

Faith Ann's face filled with delight. "I like to see a horse," she said. "My Grandpa McLean took me for a ride on his horse."

The little girl reached for Mr. Winston's hand. "Can I take a ride on your horse?"

"Oh, you can't ride this horse. She's just a baby, and she's not ready to carry people yet. But you can pet her, and she'll nuzzle your hand."

"Come inside," Mandy said to Katherine. "I got supper almost ready."

Katherine stepped across the threshold into a spotless kitchen with handcrafted maple cupboards and lintels etched with fine carving. A finely sculpted wooden bowl filled with wooden fruit sat on a table near the front window. Paul Winston, or someone in this household, certainly had a talent for woodworking.

"You folks like rabbit stew?" Without waiting for an answer, Amanda Winston grabbed the lid lifter and moved the iron plate from the firepot. She stirred the coals, shoved in a little kindling, and covered it with larger sticks. "Dishes are in the cupboard over there, Missy. You can set the table if you don't mind."

The woman frisked about the kitchen, pouring stew into a pot, heating and serving it and tidying up, until Katherine felt tired just watching her.

"Name's Katherine," she said.

Amanda picked up an old cowbell, stepped out the door, and filled the air with ragged clanging.

Before long, Faith Ann came bouncing into the room. "Mama, Mr. Winston says I can go fishin' in his lake if we stay long enough. Can we stay a while, Mama? Can we?"

She scrambled onto a bench at the backside of the table.

"I guess we'll be here for a while." Katherine smiled out of the corner of her mouth. *But not any longer than we have to,* she thought.

Minutes later, Paul had blessed the food and he leaned back, turning to Hannah. "Beach, birch, and maple, all starts with a."

Hannah's brow wrinkled. "What?"

A grin spread across Paul's face. "*A-l-l.*"

Hannah's eyes sparkled. "OK, now I got one for you. Railroad crossing without any cars; can you spell that without any *r*'s?"

Paul chewed on his lower lip in feigned confusion. "I don't know. How do you do that?"

"*T-h-a-t,*" Hannah said proudly.

"Well, you caught me on that one. By the way, what animal has the most lives?"

"I know that." Hannah's face glowed. "A cat."

"Nope, a frog. He croaks every night."

In time, Faith Ann's head began to nod, and it became apparent that the time had come to end the jokes. Frank took the little girl into the parlor and laid her on the couch, while Katherine and Hannah cleared the table, and Amanda put the teakettle on the range to heat.

"Now then," the older woman said, "let's get that little girl up to bed."

Katherine roused Faith Ann and held her upright, guiding her up the stairway to a room on the north side of the hall. An old iron bed stood in the middle of the room with a homemade chest of drawers along the north wall. Handmade lace curtains graced the windows and three shelves hung on the west wall, filled with books, toys, and small knickknacks.

"This was my girls' room, when they were at home," Amanda said. She whisked a flannel nightshirt out of a drawer and handed it to Katherine. "Faith Ann can sleep in this tonight."

Katherine pulled the shirt over Faith Ann's head and settled the child into bed. "Goodnight, sweetheart," she whispered.

Then she kissed Faith Ann on the cheek and tiptoed out of the room.

As Katherine and Amanda entered the kitchen, Hannah was finishing supper dishes, and Katherine's heart was flooded with maternal pride. She wanted to clasp her stepdaughter in a warm hug and tell her what a fine young woman she was becoming. But she knew Hannah; the girl would stiffen into an icicle, rigid and resentful.

Who do you think you are? she'd think. *You're not my mother.*

Katherine brushed a stray hair into place, not quite sure how to react.

"Hannah," she said at last, "your room is upstairs on the north side of the hall. When you're ready, you can go on up. And I'd appreciate it if you'd keep an eye on Faith Ann for me. See that she doesn't wake up in the night and get scared of the strange surroundings."

Hannah's eyes blazed. She flung the dishtowel over the rack at the end of the range.

"Yes, I'll let you know if your baby gets scared," she said with a sneer. "I'm tired now, and I'm going to bed." She hurled herself up the stairway, closing the door with a slam.

Tears beaded behind Katherine's eyes. She couldn't figure what that girl wanted. If Katherine tried to show affection, Hannah was resentful. If she remained aloof, the girl got angry. Why couldn't Hannah at least hold her temper in front of strangers?

Looking up, Katherine could see that Amanda was deeply involved with something in a drawer—folding and refolding the linens. "I wonder what the men are doing," she said.

Amanda smiled and closed the drawer. The two women moved toward the sitting room, where Paul's voice hovered in the air.

"Can you believe it?" he was saying. "They dug a tunnel right under the St. Clair River. Goes all the way from Canada to the United States."

"Yes," Frank responded. "They're doing things today I never dreamed of. And those new electric lights they have in the big cities. I heard they light up the room as if it were daylight."

"I'm not so sure that's a good idea." Paul fiddled with his shirt collar. "It just ain't right fer a man to be sittin' up half the night foolin' with this or that. How do you git your chores done in the morning? Why, it could be noon before you get out of bed."

"Well, if it weren't for men trying new things, we wouldn't have a lot of the comforts we have today—like cars and stuff."

"I ain't got no love fer cars, neither. Them speed-happy monsters go chasin' around at twenty and thirty miles an hour, spookin' livestock and creatin' all kinds of havoc. The next thing you know, the chickens won't lay anymore. They'll be too scared."

"You know," Frank said. "One of these days those horseless carriages'll be the only thing on the road. The horse and buggy will be a thing of the past."

"Well, I don't want to live to see it. When we were boys, we lived in small towns, where you knew everybody. Now you've got these great big cities like Port Huron, where you gotta have a machine to take you places."

"Paul," Mandy said, "we should probably let these folks go to bed; they've had a long day."

"I suppose you're right, but I get so dag-nabbed mad at the way the world is going these days. Everything's going to pot." Paul rose, opened the heater door and tossed in a big chunk of wood to bank the fire. "I just get to talkin' and forget to stop." Paul slipped his arm around his wife's shoulders. "Goodnight folks."

Katherine and Frank made their way upstairs to a large room that Amanda had assigned to them. There they found a home made, wooden bed covered with a brightly colored crazy-quilt. A chest of drawers stood along one wall and a dressing table with a washbowl and a pitcher of water.

"Look here." Frank reached for a pack of stationery that lay on a writing table along the north wall. "I think I'll write to Uncle Ned before I turn in."

"Well then, I think I'll try to find some extra covers for the girls."

As Frank set about writing, Katherine looked around for a likely place for blankets. She noticed an old trunk under the front window and knelt beside it. But as she lifted the lid, her heart contracted into a knot. The trunk was filled with baby clothes. She brushed her fingers over the tiny nightgowns and undershirts and diapers that would have fit Johnny perfectly. She touched the booties, the bibs, and the white stockings.

Tears welled in her eyes as she thought of Johnny. Never again would she hold her baby boy. She lifted a tiny shirt to find a wrinkled and tearstained newspaper clipping.

BABY BOY DIES OF PNEUMONIA

Benjamin Winston, age three, died this week in Meadowbrook Hospital. Benjamin had been ill for several days, before complications set in and his parents sought help from Doctor Robert Hanson. The doctor diagnosed the boy with pneumonia. Death overtook young Benjamin late Saturday. Funeral services will be held in the Christian Fellowship Church at 2:00 on Wednesday, March 24th.

Gently, Katherine replaced the trunk's contents and closed the lid, pushing back tears. Why? What kind of God was this that killed little babies? She found several quilts in the nearby closet and tossed one onto the bed where she and Frank would sleep. Then she slipped across the hall, spread the remaining quilt over her girls, and tiptoed out of the room, leaving the door ajar.

Frank hardly moved as she crawled in beside him. "Goodnight," she said.

"Goodnight," he murmured.

But Katherine didn't sleep. She lay on the bed, thinking about the trunk that sat almost within arm's reach. *Baby dies of pneumonia,* the article read. Benjamin Winston had literally choked to death. In her mind's eye, she saw him gasping and struggling for breath. She saw him red-faced and panting . . . and dying.

Resentment flared in her heart. It wasn't fair. Maybe there was no God. And so, what if there was! She wasn't sure she wanted Him in charge of her life.

Over the next week, while the McLeans stayed with the Winstons, Frank worked at the marina every day and swapped stories with Paul in the evenings.

Paul entertained Faith Ann and Hannah most days—fishing and chasing cows and caring for Josie, the newborn foal. And Katherine helped Amanda with household chores.

Time passed, *Miranda* was sold, and Katherine's family prepared to move north.

CHAPTER SIX

It was midnight two days after the sale, and Frank lay with eyes
wide open, staring at the ceiling. He looked at Katherine
sleeping quietly by his side. Was he doing the right thing?
Would she be happy in the country? What about that old stone
house? Was it suitable for a fine woman like her? Hour after
hour, Frank's mind stumbled on, until the clink of the poker
against the heater announced the arrival of daybreak.

"Mornin'," Paul said, as Frank stepped through the stairway
door. "Sleep well?"

"No, I've been awake since midnight, just lying there
thinking about things."

"I'm not surprised. Today is a big day in your life."

Frank took his coat from a nail by the kitchen door and
followed Paul to the barn. They fed the animals, milked the
cows, and cleaned Josie's stall. At eight o'clock they headed to
the house for breakfast.

And what a breakfast it was. Mandy had outdone herself
with pancakes, eggs, potatoes, ham, bacon, and applesauce.
Frank ate heartily, knowing he had a long day ahead.

"Is everything ready to go?" he said at last.

"We're ready," Hannah responded. "The clothes were
washed, ironed, and packed yesterday, and I checked my case
last night before I went to bed. But we want to say goodbye to
Josie before we leave, OK?"

"Sure, go ahead."

Frank's daughters had certainly taken to that foal. It seemed they wanted little else these days than to pet and curry her.

The girls took off on the run, while the women did the dishes and the men harnessed the horses. Frank placed Hannah's case and the sack with his family's things under the driver's bench. Finally everything was ready, and Frank called his girls. "Hannah, Faith Ann, it's time to go."

He watched, as Hannah turned, gave Josie one last pat, and started toward the house.

"C'mon, Faith Ann," she called. "We gotta go."

But Faith Ann stood unmoving, brushing her hand over Josie's mane and patting her side.

"Faith Ann!" Frank raised his voice to a commanding shout, and Faith Ann gave the foal one last pat and came running.

Frank offered a step up to Katherine and Hannah. Then he caught Faith Ann in his arms and boosted her onto the wagon. "Let's go see Uncle Ned."

"OK," Faith Ann sang, "I wanna go see Uncle Ned." Frank's soul surged with anticipation.

Paul flicked the reins, and the horses began to move.

"Wait, wait." Amanda waved her arms in a holding signal and ran toward the house.

A tremor of agitation shinnied up Frank's spine. He drummed his fingers on his knees and tapped his foot in rhythm with his beating heart. It had been a fine experience coming to know the Winstons, but now it was time to go, and he wanted to be on his way.

After what seemed an eternity, Amanda returned with a blanket draped over her arm. "Here, Katie, I want you to have this. Those trains can get pretty cold this time of year."

A rush of warmth for the older woman filled Frank's heart, as Katherine leaned over the side of the wagon in a farewell hug. "Thank you, Amanda," she said. "You folks have been most gracious. We'll never forget."

"Write when you get to Hitchcock."

"I will," Katherine promised, "and maybe I'll send you a picture of my new house."

The wagon began to move. Looking back, Frank could see Amanda waving. He knew he'd never forget the Winstons and their kindness, but his heart sang a song of hope and expectation.

At the station, Katherine and the girls boarded the train, while Frank and Paul stood on deck.

Frank's heart surged with appreciation. "You and Amanda have made these few days a really good experience." He reached for Paul's hand. "I don't know what we'd have done without you."

"Well, you just take care of yourself and your family."

The whistle blew a last warning, and Frank ran as fast as he could. He was on his way north at last and he was glad. He wanted to settle in before snowfall.

The steady cadence of iron wheels pounding endless rails melted into a distant drumbeat as the McLeans traveled north on the Pere Marquette. Katherine sat in a double-seated passenger booth, facing forward with her arm around Faith Ann's shoulders and Amanda's blanket across both their knees. Frank sat with Hannah across the compartment, deeply involved in the *Port Huron Daily Times.*

Hannah stared fixedly out the window, her attractive azure eyes engulfed by an all-too-familiar sullenness.

Oh Hannah, Katherine thought, *what am I to do with you? Will you never let down the barrier, so we can be friends? I know all too well how you hurt, because of your mother's death—how the pain goes on, year after year. I won't try to replace her. But can't we just be friends?*

Frank lowered the paper and made eye contact. "Listen to this," he said. "An early snowstorm has blown across from Canada. It is moving through Minnesota, Wisconsin, and Northern Michigan. Northern Michigan is hardest hit with twelve inches on the ground and still falling. Stores have been closed since Friday."

Katherine glanced out the window to see snowflakes dancing in the wind. "I don't like it," she said. "What if that storm hits Hitchcock? The last thing we need is a blizzard."

"You can say that again."

Faith Ann sat up. "Mama, I gotta go."

Hannah rose and reached for Faith Ann. "C'mon," she said. "I'll go with you."

The girls made their way forward, disappearing behind a tiny door in front of the car. When they returned, they took their seats, ignoring the pound, pound, pound of the train's wheels beating on the tracks.

In time, the landscape grew more populated. Open fields gave way to farms and then to communities with homes and markets. Markets grew into large shopping areas where stores clustered together in a town.

The conductor entered the car. "Ladies and gentlemen," he said and paused. "We'll be arriving at the Saginaw station within the next several minutes, and there will be a thirty-minute layover. Departure for Cadillac, Traverse City, and Boyne Falls is scheduled for eleven thirty-eight a.m. Those passengers wishing to disembark should plan to be on board by eleven-twenty."

The train began to lose speed, and minutes later it rolled into the Saginaw station.

The man across the aisle stood. "C'mon Arvilla, Grandma's waiting." The man and his young companion rose and made their way off the train.

Katherine turned to her husband. "Frank, why don't you go get us something to eat?"

"Good idea." Frank laid the newspaper aside. "What would you like?"

"Oh, I don't know. Bread and cheese might be nice . . . and maybe cookies or something."

Soon Katherine was alone with Faith Ann and Hannah. Snow drifted around the car's windows, and Katherine could see patches of white clinging to buildings and boardwalks. Hannah stared out the window, intent on some unknown attraction.

"Hannah," Katherine said, "are you looking forward to Hitchcock?" "Not really."

"Won't it be great to have our own home again?" "I suppose."

"Do you think we should buy that stone house your pa keeps talking about, or should we build a house of our own?"

"I dunno."

Hannah never took her eyes off the stores across the street, and Katherine stopped trying. She reached for the *Port Huron Times,* mindlessly scanning the front page.

Before long, an older couple boarded the train, followed by a younger man and woman with two small children. Several rough looking men—probably lumberjacks—took their places, and a tall, lean man came aboard carrying a leather bag that appeared to contain books or tools.

Dropping the bag into an empty compartment at the cold end of the car, he took a seat near the other woodsmen, grinning as if he'd just learned some deep secret. Somehow, the turn of his lip reminded Katherine of Clive Isaman, Faith Ann's father. She remembered their first date—July 1, 1891 at the Dominion Day fireworks.

They sat on one of Mama Sally's old patchwork quilts spread out on the ground about halfway up the hillside. One moment the sky over Lake Huron had been dark and empty, and the next moment the whole area lit up in fiery display. Near the end of the evening, Clive had taken advantage of the darkness to pull Katherine close, kissing her gently but with passion. She could remember that kiss as if it were yesterday.

A year and a half later, on the night before Clive went "up for Jackman" to work in the lumber camp, she'd lost her virginity.

Clive never came back, and he never knew about Faith Ann.

Soon all the passengers were seated, and the conductor entered the car. He made his way to a small heater near the front entrance, opened the door, stirred the coals, and tossed in several small sticks from a nearby woodbox, adding several larger pieces for long-term burning.

With the fire tended, he turned to the people. "We'll be leaving Saginaw directly. There's a bad snowstorm north of us, and we're likely to encounter drifts along the tracks. If we do, the engineer will open the throttle and try to ram through, so the ride may be turbulent at times. Passengers should remain seated unless a move is of utmost importance."

The locomotive belched, a puff of steam rolled past the window, and the Pere Marquette began to move. It gathered speed, puffing down the tracks on its way north.

The train traveled deeper and deeper into untamed timberland, snaking its way into the eerie darkness that settled into the territory. Surrounding trees grew large and thick, crowding nearer and nearer the tracks, until it seemed one could almost reach out and touch them. Giant trunks stretched upward past the windows of the car—trunks so big you couldn't reach your arms around them.

Then, in a moment's time, they broke into bright sunlight, and Katherine looked out on a broad expanse of empty, snow-covered stump-land. Several high, limbless trees left behind by loggers rose out of the snow, weather worn and rotting.

"Minds me of that witherin' blast of 1893," one of the lumberjacks hollered. "Wadin' in that stuff up to our waists, we was. We was a-cuttin' them stumps about ten feet tall. Old Danglin' Jim Fosset went out one day, a-lookin' fer a canthook and didn't come back fer two weeks. Lost in a whiteout, he was."

The jacks fell to talking among themselves, each one trying to outdo the others with his own fantastic story.

The man with the compelling smile looked at Katherine and shrugged, as if to say, "Who knows?"

Several times the train came upon drifts that covered the tracks, but the engineer simply picked up speed and rammed his way through. The coaches slammed together, tossing passengers this way and that. And when the snow settled, the train had gone its way. Then, late in the afternoon, the locomotive began to lose speed. The Pere Marquette ground to a stop.

Katherine looked at Frank and Frank looked at Katherine. Both Frank and Katherine looked at Hannah with eyebrows raised in puzzlement. The couple across the aisle grumbled about lost time, and one of the tree fellers erupted into a blast of expletives.

"What's a-goin' on with them buzzards up there? Can't they handle a piddlin' little snowstorm? Why, I seen worse'n this in the middle of spring, when I was nothin' but a pup. I can remember . . ."

The conductor entered the car and stood waiting until the tirade ceased. "Ladies and gentlemen," he said at last, "there's a big drift across the tracks. We've backed down the tracks, so we can increase our speed and hit it full force. You should gather any loose items and secure them."

He glanced at the McLeans. "And be sure to hang onto small children."

He walked out of the car, and Frank reached across the compartment for Faith Ann. "We're going to hit a big bump. Lean on me and I'll hold you tight."

Momentarily the train began to move forward, slowly at first and gathering speed as it went. *Puff, puff, puff, puff.* Iron wheels pounded unyielding rails. *Clickety-clack, clickety-clack, clickety-clack.* Steam billowed around windows, nearly obscuring the countryside. Faster and faster went the Pere Marquette. *Clickety, clickety, clickety, clickety.* The whistle screamed, *wooow, wooow, wooow, wooow.* Trees raced by like feathers in the wind.

And the train rammed the barrier.

Windows clattered and the little heater shook. The wood box skated across the floor, tossing sticks here and there. Great chunks of hard-packed snow went flying past windows like God-made snowballs.

"Ooohh, look outside," Hannah called, "snow everywhere! What a sight!"

Then, without skipping a beat, the ride grew smooth. The Pere Marquette rolled steadily northward, pounding the tracks with a steady beat.

The train rolled along all afternoon, until at last, the conductor appeared in the doorway. "We should arrive in Hitchcock in about ten minutes. We'll stop just long enough to allow passengers to disembark and we'll be on our way."

Katherine looked outside to see a sunny sky with a brisk wind that shook the trees. Her heart began to flutter.

"Please God," she whispered. "Let Uncle Ned be waiting at the tracks."

When the Pere Marquette stopped, Frank wrapped Amanda's blanket around Faith Ann and lifted her into his arms. Hannah picked up her case, Katherine reached for the bag that held the family's clothing, and the McLeans moved toward the exit.

As Katherine stepped off the train, she turned back to see the tall, thin lumberman. He smiled and nodded goodbye, and a strange, inexplicable warmth rippled through her system. Shaking it off, Katherine turned and stepped into six inches of snow.

Standing with her family, she watched the Pere Marquette as it disappeared into the dark, virgin lumber fields. They were alone now. Only the rails and a narrow opening broke the wall of trees. She swallowed hard to prevent her discouragement from rising to the surface.

So now what? Where was Uncle Ned?

CHAPTER SEVEN

Frank stepped off the coach into ankle-deep snow, peering down the tracks where the train had just gone. A trail of white extended from one end of the passageway to the other with trees crowding close on either side. In the woods, he could hear the snap and crackle of tree branches giving way under the heavy weight of snow they carried. But it was another sound that caught his attention—the crunch of animal feet on the forest floor. Maybe it was Uncle Ned coming for them with his sleigh. Did he dare to hope?

Faith Ann shivered in his arms, and Katherine and Hannah stood in the snow, waiting for Frank to do something. They hadn't any boots, and Frank knew their feet must be nearly frozen.

What had he done, bringing his family out into this wilderness? If anything happened to them, he'd never forgive himself. He plunged forward toward the shelter of the forest.

Then the sound of whistling wafted on the air. Yes, he was sure of it. Someone was whistling "Yankee Doodle."

And a horse burst through the trees, hauling a dilapidated old sleigh. The black paint that once glistened on its homemade cab was now rough and peeling, the curtains that draped the windows were worn and ragged, and the entire sleigh was badly in need of repair. But it could not have been more beautiful if it were the queen's royal coach.

"Whoa, Maud," called the man on the driver's bench.

The rig stopped, and a wiry little man in a heavy winter coat and pants jumped to the ground. Wresting a shovel from clips on the side of the sleigh, he cleared a path, coming ever nearer to Frank and his family.

"Are you the McLeans?" he called.

"That we are," Frank responded. "I'm Frank McLean and this here's my family. We've come from Ontario, looking for my Uncle Ned."

"I be Oren Gallagher," the man said. "Ned said to take you to Hitchcock's general store. He's planning to meet you when he hears the train go by."

Frank nodded toward his family. "This is my wife, Katherine, and the young lady there is our daughter, Hannah." He patted Faith Ann's back. "And this is our youngest, Faith Ann."

Faith Ann lifted her face, peeked at Mr. Gallagher, and then buried it again in Frank's neck.

"Well, let's git movin'." Oren Gallagher offered his arm to Katherine, and then reached out for Hannah.

Hannah took his hand and mounted the steps. "Thank you, Mr. Gallagher."

Frank smiled at the air of nobility in his daughter's voice. He boosted Faith Ann into the shelter of the cab. Then he took a seat beside Oren on the driver's bench.

"Giddap," Oren called, and the sleigh glided over the narrow, two-track road into the woods.

Oren pointed to a large, rough-hewn structure with tarpaper roof and sides. "See that big building over there? That's Paul Decker's sawmill. He ain't got no wife or kids, so he just hangs around most o' the time. An' the little gray house over there? That's my place."

The sleigh turned south out of the woods, and Oren nodded toward the rear. "If we'd a-turned north here you'd see a lake at the bottom of that ravine back there. It's called Little Birch Lake."

Frank turned to see a narrow lane snaking into the ever-present forest.

"And about a half-mile farther is Big Birch Lake. Big Birch has got some of the best bass and catfish around these parts."

Oren kept a running conversation with himself. "And there's a swimmin' hole there, too. It's kinda small, but it's got a fair beach, and there's a bath house and a privy."

The road widened, leaving an open swath about a mile deep on either side. An old stone house stood on the right with a barn and a tool shed, all unpainted and in need of repair. Deep snow covered everything.

"That there's the Beasley place," Oren said. "They say when Angus and Gretchen first came here, back in the eighteen fifties, they cut the trees and burned 'em to make room for the farm. If they'd a-sold them logs, they could a-got rich, but there wasn't any roads or mills in them days, and no one ever thought o' sellin' the trees. So they just burned 'em—hundreds o' dollars worth o' trees."

Oren flicked the reins, and the horse picked up speed.

"They never had but one son, the Beasleys, and when the grandson inherited the place a few years back, he went off to the lumber camps and got hisself killed. His widow was so unsettled by the whole thing, she just took the kids and moved on down to Grand Rapids, where her folks were. Place reverted to the state, I s'pose."

"Maybe that's the house Uncle Ned mentioned," Frank said. "He wrote about an old stone house that was abandoned. Said maybe I could buy it for back taxes and fix it up."

"Wouldn't be the least surprised. These old houses, they just go to rot and ruin when folks abandon 'em. Wood frame rots and falls apart, leavin' the stone walls a-standin' there like ghosts in a graveyard."

The road turned west, past a blacksmith shop on the left. "And that there's Hans Kubek's place," Oren said. "He's a purty good smith, if I do say so. Does all the local folks' horses 'n' things. And some o' the nearby jobbers, too."

Frank smiled and nodded, wondering if the Beasley place would be available.

"And right up there's Hitchcock's."

Ahead on the right, Frank could see an unpainted building made of rough-sawn lumber. An overhang extended from the eaves, and a boardwalk lay along the front. A sign hung over the steps, hand painted in bright red lettering: Hitchcock's General Store.

"Sam, this here's Ned's family," Oren said as they opened the door. "Ned said to bring 'em by here."

A tall, thin man with straight, black hair and moustache came around the counter with his hand extended.

"Pleased to meet you folks," he said, gripping Frank's hand like a long time friend and neighbor. "Ned mentioned you'd be by."

"Thank you, Oren," Frank called as Oren exited the store. Frank loosened Amanda's blanket from Faith Ann's shoulders and put the little girl in a chair near the heater.

"I'm Frank McLean, and this is my wife, Katherine. That's my daughter, Hannah, and the younger one here is Faith Ann. We'd like to get to Uncle Ned's place as soon as possible."

"I'm Sam Hitchcock," the man said. "Ned'll have heard the train when it went by. He'll be along shortly."

Frank looked at the big clock on the wall. Its pendulum rocked back and forth behind a glass front, with the words Seth Thomas embossed on it in gold. It was eighteen minutes after four. Twenty minutes later, the sound of snorting horses filled the air, and footsteps resounded on the porch.

"Well, Frankie," Uncle Ned called as he entered the store. "I see you finally made it. How was the trip?"

He clapped Frank on the back and reached out in a hearty handshake.

"Uncle Ned, it's good to see you!"

Frank's heart soared with the realization that he'd reached his destination. "The trip was long and tiring . . . and a little scary when the train got stopped by a big drift. But the engineer just rammed his way through, and here we are."

Ned laughed. "It's pretty deep out there, all right. I don't know why it had to be this way. We don't usually get snow like this so early in the fall."

"Well, we're glad to be here anyway."

Frank introduced Uncle Ned to his family, and then the McLeans took their leave on the last leg of their journey to a new life.

They traveled down Birch Lake Road, past a small church on the right, and turned onto a narrow country lane. A small cabin nestled under two big chestnut trees stood at the end of the track.

Katherine's breath caught in her throat as Uncle Ned's cabin came into view. How in the world would they fit two families into that tiny little place? Boys or young men might sleep in the haymow if the weather were nice, but not her girls. This was just not a suitable arrangement.

"Whoa," Uncle Ned called and the sleigh came to a stop. Frank hopped to the ground and reached up for Faith Ann. As Katherine and Hannah climbed down, the door to the house flew open, and a little woman about five-feet, four-inches tall stepped outside with arms outstretched and a smile that seemed to spread from ear to ear.

Frank leaned close to Katherine and whispered, "That's my Aunt Mae."

Aunt Mae might have added pounds over the years, but she certainly looked fit to Katherine. Her gray hair, which lay close to her face in tightly controlled waves, was pulled into a bun at the back of her neck. She wore a blue gingham apron across her entire front.

"It's great to see you, Frankie," she cried. She threw her arms around her nephew. "You're lookin' real good."

Frank hugged his aunt and patted her on the back. "It's good to see you too, Aunt Mae."

Looking up, Aunt Mae turned a smile in Katherine's direction. "And I guess you're Frankie's wife." She held out a welcoming hand. "Frankie, you got yourself a real handsome woman there."

Aunt Mae led the way inside, where a large kettle of chicken and dumplings simmered on the range.

"Supper's ready, so if you folks are hungry, we can eat," Aunt Mae said as she spooned dumplings onto a platter.

When all was ready and the family had taken their places at the table, Uncle Ned bowed his head.

"Lord, we thank you for your bounty, and for your hand of protection as our family traveled. Now please bless this food to the strengthening of our bodies. Amen."

Frank squeezed Katherine's hand under the table. "Uncle Ned always said, *'You don't have to plead with God for Him to bless you.'"*

After supper Aunt Mae leaped to her feet. She cleared the table before Katherine had time to think. She splashed hot water into the dishpan and whisked the dishes into it. It took both Katherine and Hannah wiping at top speed to keep up with the woman.

"C'mon," Aunt Mae said when the kitchen was clean. "I'll show you to your beds.

Katherine followed Aunt Mae, dismayed at the energy of this aggressive woman. Entering the room, she found it packed with furniture. A double bed stood along one wall with a divan opposite. A narrow aisle allowed passage between the two. A fireplace filled the east wall, leaving just enough space to walk around the foot of the bed to a door on the far side of the room.

"You and Frankie can sleep in the double bed," Aunt Mae said. "And Faith Ann will use the couch."

She pulled back the quilt on the divan. "There you go, young lady. Now, where's your nightgown?"

"Actually, we only brought a few essentials," Katherine said. "She's been sleeping in her underwear."

"Well, let's see if we can find her a nice clean shirt or something."

Aunt Mae whisked down the narrow walkway between the bed and the divan. She followed the pathway around the foot of the bed past the fireplace and exited through the door on the north side of the room. Katherine took a seat on the couch and pulled Faith Ann close as if to claim ownership.

Soon Aunt Mae came bustling back into the room. "Here we are. I got this old undershirt. It should do the job for now."

She nudged Katherine aside and began unfastening Faith Ann's dress, and Katherine bristled. "I can take care of Faith Ann if you'll just . . . ."

But Aunt Mae was off and running. In no time she had Faith Ann swimming in Uncle Ned's shirt. Katherine found herself resenting this overbearing woman who made her feel like a little kid.

Finally, Aunt Mae pulled the covers over Faith Ann's shoulders and sat beside her, humming a little tune.

Faith Ann drifted into sleep. "C'mon," the older woman said, rising to her feet. "I'll show you Hannah's room."

She picked up the lamp and bustled through the doorway. Katherine hesitated, leaning down to kiss her baby on the cheek.

"Mama's here, sweetheart," she whispered. Then she followed Aunt Mae out of the room. A lump lodged in her chest and, try as she might, she couldn't displace it. It was good of Aunt Mae to make room in her home, but how long could Katherine live in this tiny house with that overbearing woman?

Aunt Mae led the way at breakneck speed through the dining room. "C'mon Hannah. We'll show you to your room."

The little procession passed through the kitchen and into the pantry, where a bed had been placed under the only window in the room. Shelves of kitchen supplies covered three walls and large bags of staples sat on the floor. A butter churn sat near the doorway.

"It'll be close, but it's the only place we could think of." Hannah crawled across the bed on her knees and peered out the window.

"Oh, don't do that," Aunt Mae snapped. "It's too hard on the feather tick."

Hannah turned quickly and sat on the edge of the bed.

Katherine's lips squeezed into a thin line, creating a barrier against what she might say.

Later that night, Katherine lay on her bed with eyes wide open. Faith Ann slept restlessly on the divan not four feet away.

"Frank," Katherine said, "this is never going to work. We can't stay in this crowded little house."

"You're right, Katie. We'll find a place real soon."

"Let's go take a look at that stone house tomorrow. If it turns out we can't use it, at least we'll know what it's like, and we can begin to think about something else."

"OK." Frank said no more, and he soon fell asleep.

But Katherine lay awake listening to the sounds of the night. She thought about Seth and about Johnny. And she wondered where her future led.

CHAPTER EIGHT

It was mid-afternoon, the sun was shining, and the snow was melting away, as those early snows are wont to do. Hannah and Katherine sat in the sleigh, and Frank sat on the driver's bench with his uncle. Faith Ann had remained at the cabin with Aunt Mae. "You go on over to the Beasley place and look around," Aunt Mae had said. "I don't need to see it. Faith Ann can stay here with me and make cookies."

Katherine's heart wrenched. How could she have been so upset with Frank's aunt? The woman had been a big help when she was needed most. She simply didn't realize how frustrating it was to be pushed aside all the time.

"Look, Hannah," Katherine said as they passed a dome-like hill on the left. "Did you ever see the ground rise out of nowhere like that?"

Hannah stiffened. "There are a lot of things I'm seeing these days that I never saw before." The wall of ice between Katherine and Hannah almost crackled in its intensity.

Soon the sleigh glided over a bridge, and Uncle Ned reined in the horses.

"This here's Parson Tibbs' Creek," he said. "It rises from a spring, about halfway up that hill, and it flows all year round, even on the coldest winter days."

Uncle Ned pointed up the incline. "Can you see the little building standing under the oak tree over there?"

Katherine looked up to see a little white chapel with its steeple rising toward the clouds.

"That's Parson Tibbs' church," Uncle Ned explained. "The parson's been here almost as long as Sam Hitchcock, I guess. They came to the area when this was a logging village for the Grahong lumber camp. The hill the church sets on is Parson's Dome. They say it was left when the glacier receded after the ice age."

Katherine shook her head. She never did understand how those scientists figured out things like that.

As they rounded the dome, a large building came in sight on the left.

"That's the Grange Hall," Uncle Ned called out. "It serves as a meeting place for town meetings and stuff like that."

They passed Hitchcock's General Store and turned north by Kubek's blacksmith shop toward Birch Lake. Before long, the sleigh glided into the driveway at the old fieldstone house. It was a single story building with deep-set windows that overlooked wide sills, which might have been used for flower boxes, or for heating a jug of sun tea, or maybe a shelf for cooling freshly baked apple pies. Maybe the ledge had served to store a pail of huckleberries until Mrs. Beasley could get around to canning or making jam.

Katherine stepped down onto the slushy ground and approached the house. She was about to peek through the window, when Frank called out from behind the place.

"Hey, come see what I found."

Katherine made her way around back, where Frank stood in the woodshed with the door wide open.

"I just turned the knob," he said.

Katherine mounted the steps and entered a dust-covered but otherwise spacious, well-kept kitchen. An old iron range stood on her right, facing a wall of beautifully crafted, handmade cupboards.

A small utility table stood against the west wall, with a window looking out over the back yard. The curtains over the glass were faded and falling apart. The place needed cleaning, but it showed real promise. Katherine's heart surged.

Leading the way now, she pushed through the double doors into the parlor, and recoiled in disappointment. Crumbling plaster littered the floor, and bare strips of lath hung exposed on walls and ceilings. Some animal had gnawed its way into the sitting room, leaving a hole in the north wall where ice and snow had blown in. A brown stain extended halfway to the ceiling, and a window was broken. Bird droppings lay everywhere on rotting floorboards that creaked and threatened to give way.

There was no way Katherine's family could move into this house before Frank came home in the spring. Unbidden tears stung the back of her eyes. With aching heart she turned and walked outside.

A week had passed and it was mid-November. The snows had begun in earnest, and Frank and Jasper needed to leave that morning for the lumber camp. Aunt Mae had found an old flour sack and put a hem in the open end.

"Here's a sack to use for your turkey," she said.

A rope had been strung through the hem of the sack and, when it was filled with Frank's belongings it could be pulled tight and slung over his shoulder for easy transport.

Katherine laid out two pairs of heavy winter underwear, some wool socks, and a couple of shirts—flannel and wool—because temperatures in the woods could fall well below zero.

Frank pulled out his razor, some shaving soap, and a comb. These he put in a cigar box he'd gotten from Sam Hitchcock.

Uncle Ned entered the room with a handful of red and blue neckerchiefs.

"Here, Frank, you'll need these."

Frank stuffed the cigar box and bandanas into the bag with his other things. That almost completed the list Jasper had given him.

"You should have a needle and thread," Aunt Mae said. "And here's some cough syrup," Katherine added.

All the while, Hannah stood nearby looking lost and alone. She held out a handkerchief she'd taken from her case.

"Here, Pa," she said at last. "Take this to the camp with you, so you'll think of me sometimes."

A lump lodged in Frank's throat. He grabbed his daughter in an emotional hug, as he hadn't done in many months.

"But spring will come before you know it, and we can be a family again." His voice cracked as he spoke.

Hannah stepped back, looking up at Frank with teary eyes. "I'll miss you, Pa."

"I'll miss you too, Hannah."

Frank gulped, trying to deny the tears that forced themselves forward. He lifted Faith Ann into his arms, held her close, and kissed her cheek. "And I'll miss my little dumplin'."

Putting the child down, he turned to his wife. Katherine fell into his arms, and he held her close for many long minutes. "I'll try to come home for Christmas," he whispered.

Katherine looked up with a smile that belied the pain in her eyes. "I'll be waiting."

Frank kissed his dear one for the last time, slung his turkey over his shoulder, and began the two-mile trek to Jasper's house.

"Frank, be careful. Don't get yourself hurt."

Frank turned to see Katherine standing in the chilly air. She blew him a kiss.

Katherine watched her husband's departing form as it receded into the distance. Cloaked in his mackinaw and gray McMillan trousers, which Jasper had suggested he hack off at the calf, he rounded the bend at the end of the lane and turned onto Birch Lake Road. His boots with ten-inch leather tops covered his legs, and the sheepskin insoles that had been inserted would help protect his feet from frostbite. The sight of him burned into Katherine's memory.

Soon Frank would arrive at Jasper's house. He'd join the camp crew, and Katherine wouldn't see him again until

Christmas—or maybe not until spring. She swallowed the lump in her throat and went inside.

That evening Katherine retired for the night, alone in their double bed.

The next morning she awoke, dressed, and went to the kitchen. There she found Aunt Mae bustling about, looking for something.

"Katherine, have you seen my blue granite kettle?" the older woman asked. "I left it right here on the cabinet."

"Check Hannah's room," Katherine responded. "I think I saw Uncle Ned carry it in there."

"Oh, in the pantry."

Katherine didn't fail to notice the edge in Aunt Mae's voice. It was her pantry, not Hannah's room. There must be a way, Katherine thought. There just had to be a way she could move out of this house before spring.

Frank spent the night at Camp Rifkin, the base unit for Waterhouse Lumber Company. At one time Rifkin had been a bustling, productive lumber camp, but today it was maintained by Molly and Burgess Walker as a supply and support unit for the Company's outlying facilities.

Luc DuBois had been at Rifkin for several weeks already, scouting the area and laying out plans for the DuBois camp. Swampers had cleared the site and hewers had cut and decked logs to be used for buildings. Roof and floor lumber had been brought in from the mill. Today the crew would erect a village in the woods.

The triangle rang, and Frank climbed out of his bunk. He thrust his leg into his McMillans, and pulled on his shirt and boots. He pulled his suspenders over his shoulders, grabbed his mackinaw, and left the bunkhouse. He entered the cook shanty to find the teamsters walking out the door. It was their job to rise early, eat breakfast, and then feed and curry the horses. By the time the rest of the crew had finished eating, the team should be ready to go to work.

Frank took a seat next to Jasper and Emma and then filled his plate with Molly's good pancakes and pork sausage. Few individuals were more important to a lumber camp than a good cook, and Molly was one of the best.

"Mornin' Frank," Jasper said as Frank took his seat. His voice was a quiet murmur.

"Mornin'," Frank responded.

Although the usual lumber camp rule demanded absolute silence during meals, it was not strictly observed at Rifkin. After the long, lonely summer months, Molly was quite ready to visit with her guests and to listen to their conversation.

The jacks spoke very little, however, and breakfast was downed in about fifteen minutes. Then Luc DuBois rose from his place at the head of the table.

"Let's get with it, fellers," he called. "We got work to do."

The crew rose as a unit, exited the cook shanty, and headed down the tote road toward the place that would become Camp DuBois.

At the site, the team moved the horses into position beside a pile of logs. Hiram Breen tailed down the first log and it rolled off the deck. Lev Ivanov toggled it to the whiffletree, Klause Bruner yelled, "Giddap," and the horses hauled the log into position to build a frame for the bunkhouse.

Almost before the horses had stopped, Klause released the chain, dropping the log onto the ground. Bert Parsons and Tom Malenkoff maneuvered the log into place with their canthooks, and other jacks packed dirt along its sides to hold it firm.

With the log secured, the hewers flew into action, cutting notches at each end of the log to make a corner coupling. By this time, the second log had been dropped in place, and Bert and Tom secured it at right angles. Jacks packed mud along its base, and hewers notched its ends. Soon four logs lay coupled together in a rectangle, forming the base for a bunkhouse. The building would be about twenty feet wide by thirty feet long.

When the base was ready, skid ramps were leaned against it. Log after log skidded up the ramps until the bunkhouse stood about seven or eight feet high.

"Bring in the ridge pole," Klause called.

By mid-afternoon, one crew was nailing rough boards onto the roof, while another chinked cracks with long, V-shaped strips of wood. These were then covered with mud to seal the cracks.

Frank marveled at the speed and precision with which these men could throw up a building. It was like a dance, where each man moved in perfect precision with all the others.

Inside, Hans and Fritz packed the cracks with swamp moss, while Frank and Jasper built bunks. Finally, dusk settled and the triangle rang out for supper. Frank was tired and hungry, but tonight he would sleep on a new bunk with a fine layer of straw for a mattress and a heater in the middle of the room.

Over the following days, the men built a cook shanty for Jasper and Emma with a root cellar near the back door. They built a barn, a blacksmith cabin, a filer's shed, an office for Luc DuBois with an adjacent wanigan or camp store for Frank. And another unmentionable building, a long shed-like shelter with a log to sit over, while the men relieved themselves of their bodies' cast-off comestibles.

When the encampment was complete, Camp DuBois would begin to fill with lumberjacks. It would be Frank's job to stock the wanigan and to record the date of each jack's arrival, along with the position he would fill. The first two names on the books were Jasper McLean, straw boss, and Emma McLean, cook.

Hannah sat on the edge of her bed, an empty heartache gnawing at her soul. The bed, a wooden box with a network of ropes and a feather tick, took up the entire end of the tiny room where she slept. The walls were filled with crocks of flour and sugar and salt. There were pots and pans and colanders, as well as food grinders and apple peelers and cabbage graters. Her bedroom was Aunt Mae's pantry, and it looked like one.

She leaned over the bed and pushed up the sash to open the window. The air was cold, and she'd have to close the window soon, but for now she savored the invigorating vibrancy of the outdoors.

She reached under the bed, pulled out her case, and fingered through its contents to find the mint green hand towels Grandma Sally had given her, the doilies from Millie, and four blue napkin holders from Grandma McLean. Tucked among the towels was Great-grandmother Hamlin's brooch. Hannah brushed her fingers over the initials on the back of her precious heirloom. She wondered how Grandmother Hamlin would have felt about this desolate place.

"You were named after your great-grandmother Hamlin," Grandma McLean had said. "And she would want you to have her brooch."

That was a little over a month ago, and in that time Hannah's whole world had changed. She'd left her friends in Bounding to come out to this awful place where she didn't know a soul. The only thing she knew was the dull, empty ache that filled her bones.

Tucking the brooch inside her case, she pulled out a pad of paper and a pen. Then she slid her treasures back under the bed and began to write.

> *Dear Grandma,*
>
> *We've been in Hitchcock for a while now and I feel lonely a lot of the time. Mostly I've been cooped up in Uncle Ned's house, because I don't have any friends in town. There's another girl in school who is near my age. Her name is Angela, and she's in seventh grade, a year younger than me. She lives on a farm out beyond Uncle Ned's house.*
>
> *Uncle Ned is OK and so is Aunt Mae, I guess, but it seems like Aunt Mae wants to run everything. I get tired of being bossed around about every little thing.*
>
> *Uncle Ned's house is pretty small, and we are crowded, so I sleep in the pantry. It's dark and close in here, and I'll be glad if I ever get my own room.*

The town is named after Sam Hitchcock, who runs the store. There's a Grange Hall, a sawmill, a blacksmith shop, and a church and school. Oh yes, and there's a post office. The post office is in Hitchcock's.

Pa plans to buy a lathe when we have the money. Then he'll rent space at the mill. He'll make canthooks and peaveys for lumberjacks. Canthooks are poles with hooks and a blunt end that the lumberjacks use to move logs. And peaveys are the same, except they have a sharp point on the end.

For now, though, Pa has gone into the woods with Cousin Jasper to build the camp where they will work. Pa'll be keeping track of the camp records mostly, and Uncle Jasper will be the straw boss. Uncle Jasper's wife, Emma, will be the cook. They'll be gone most of the winter.

Oh, Grandma, what'll I do without Pa? I miss him so. Katherine's so wrapped up in Faith Ann that she doesn't know I'm alive. She never notices the good things I do. She's not my mother and I'm trapped with her. Sometimes I think I'll just run away.

I miss you a lot.
Your granddaughter, Hannah

Hannah folded the letter and laid it on the shelf Aunt Mae had cleared for her. She'd take it to Hitchcock's as soon as she got a chance.

CHAPTER NINE

Lift, fold, push . . . lift, fold, push.

Katherine stood alone in the kitchen punching out bread dough. "Be sure to put the bread in the warming oven to rise," she muttered. "And don't forget to cover it with a wet towel."

Why couldn't Aunt Mae give her credit for a little sense? She didn't need that woman to tell her how to bake bread.

Katherine flung the finished dough into a pan, covered it with a wet towel, and shoved it into the warming oven. "There, Aunt Mae. The bread is set to rise."

It seemed to Katherine that Aunt Mae was constantly hovering over her. *Set the table this way; fold the towels that way; stack the dishes like this.* Aunt Mae was kind and generous and very capable, and Katherine had high regard for her. But couldn't she just give Katherine credit for having a brain?

"When Frank comes home at Christmas, we'll have to find a place to live," she went on, "or I'll go stark raving mad."

A rustle in the pantry reminded Katherine that Hannah was yet to be dealt with as well. Ever since Frank left, the girl had been in a stir. It seemed no one could reach her.

"Hannah," she called, "will you go down to the cellar and get a jar of chicken for supper tonight?"

Hannah flounced out of the pantry with a scowl on her face. "What did you say you wanted?"

"Hannah, for crying out loud, snap out of it! Your pa is gone and there's nothing we can do about it. I don't like it any better than you do."

Hannah stared into Katherine's eyes with a look of pure resentment. "It's all your fault. If it wasn't for you, I'd be back on the farm with Grandma McLean. I wouldn't be forced to sleep in a closet full of strainers and choppers and garlic buds. I'd have my friends, and I'd be able to do things on my own once in a while."

She stomped across the room to the cellar door that lay flat with the floor. She slipped her finger into a hole in its corner and lifted the board. As she climbed down the ladder, Katherine could hear her grumbling. "I hate you," she muttered. "I hope . . ." the words were swallowed up in the perpetual gray haze that existed in the earthen hole that was the cellar.

When Hannah returned to the kitchen, Katherine was ready with a calculated response.

"Hannah, what would you like me to do? We're here, and there's no changing it. That's just the way it is."

"I don't expect you to do a thing."

Hannah shoved the quart of chicken onto the counter and stomped off to the pantry. "Like you said, we're here and there's nothing we can do about it."

What's the use? Katherine thought. *Hannah's just as unhappy as I am. Maybe Frank can talk to her if he comes home for Christmas.* She untied her apron, pulled it over her head, and laid it on a chair.

What if Frank didn't come home for the holiday? She brushed her hand across the front of her dress and smoothed her hair. She didn't want to even think about that possibility.

"Faith Ann, are you ready to go to Hitchcock's with me?"

In the pantry Katherine could hear Hannah slamming things around. "Faith Ann, are you coming?"

Faith Ann bounced into the kitchen. "I'm ready," she sang. "Can I get a peppermint stick from Mister Sam?" "Yes, I'm sure there'll be a peppermint stick for you. And you can bring one home for Hannah, too."

Katherine threw on her coat and helped Faith Ann into the new snowsuit Aunt Mae had picked up for her at Hitchcock's.

Taking the little girl by the hand, she walked outside into a brisk, cold morning. She pulled a scarf over her little girl's face and hurried down the lane.

"Good morning, Sam," she said later, as she pushed through the door. "How are things?"

"Oh, fair to middlin', I guess. What can I do for you, Katherine?"

"I just came by for the mail."

Sam pulled a stack of letters from a postal box on the wall and shuffled through them. "Well, let's see, there's something here from Frank."

Sam paused, thumbing through the letters in his hand. "And here's one for Hannah and a couple for Ned."

He handed the letters to Katherine. "And look here, Faith Ann, what I have for you."

Sam pulled a peppermint stick from a jar on the counter and dropped it into the little girl's hand.

Katherine chose a chair near the heater and isolated herself mentally. She slipped her finger under the flap and opened the letter.

> *Dear Katherine,*
>
> *Missing you, as always. I don't have a lot of time to sit around and think about things, though, because I have to keep track of all the jacks' time, as well as ordering all of the supplies for the camp and filling various other duties.*
>
> *Jasper and Emma stay in the cook shanty. Emma's a good cook, but they don't have cookees to help in the kitchen, so Jasper and I stand in most of the time. The chances look good for a few days at home, come Christmas. I'm looking forward to it.*
>
> *I really like Luc DuBois. He's the camp boss, and he's tough as nails but not unreasonable. He and I went to Petoskey last weekend to order supplies. I checked on a lathe while we were there, and they have some good ones for*

eighteen or twenty dollars. Lord willing, I'll be
an independent businessman by this time next
year.

Hoping to be home for Christmas,
Frank.

Katherine's eyes misted over. She could hardly wait for the holidays. While he was home, they'd talk about a place of their own.

As she sat perusing the letter, the front door opened and closed.

"Sam, I'm going to need a new pair of boots, size ten and a half, for my next trek, and I'll need some woolen mittens. Give me a bag of apples, and I'd like a sack of candy. I have a young friend that I'll be seeing very soon."

Katherine's concentration was disrupted. There was something familiar about that voice. She looked up to see Faith Ann standing near the counter beside a tall, rangy-looking man with cocoa brown hair curling around his ears. His red-and-black plaid coat hung over a pair of McMillan trousers. A scabbard hung from his belt with a knife handle sticking out.

Faith Ann lifted her chin with her usual childlike curiosity. "Where ya goin', mister?"

The man leaned down, smiling. "Well, how do you do, little lady? I'm going for a long walk in the woods."

"My name's Faith Ann. What's your name?"

"My name's Clive, Clive Isaman."

Katherine almost choked.

"And I have a little niece over in Canada that's just about your age. She likes suckers. Do you like suckers?" Clive pulled a sucker out of the candy jar and held it out to Faith Ann.

"Thank you, Mister Clive, but I already got a peppermint stick from Mister Sam."

"That's OK. You can save the sucker for later."

Clive tucked the candy into Faith Ann's pocket and turned his attention to Sam. "Here's the list, Sam. If you'll pack up these things, I'll be by for 'em next Wednesday."

Katherine sat dumbfounded. Should she walk up and say hello or should she hide behind the heater?

"My mama's right over here. Wanna come see her?"

"Sure, I'd love to meet your mama."

Faith Ann grabbed Clive by the hand and dragged him toward Katherine's chair.

Well, that was that. It was going to happen whether Katherine wanted it or not.

She rose to her feet, smiling. "Hello, Clive." Her heart beat a wild rhythm, and her knees felt like they would surely melt.

"Katherine! Katherine Baines. How in the world did you get way out here in this underdeveloped territory?"

"We came here this fall." Tension tugged at Katherine's nerves. "Our house in Bounding burned down and my husband's uncle said there was work out here. So we just packed up and came over."

Clive turned. "Sam, this beautiful lady was my girlfriend years ago, when I was nothin' but a sprout."

A big smile spread across Sam's face. "Well, what do you know?" He dropped a pair of boots on the counter. "These folks are new here in Hitchcock. They're staying out west of town with relatives."

Clive's face blossomed into a broad grin. "Katherine, you're just as beautiful as ever. And is this delightful little girl yours?"

"Yes, she's my daughter." Katherine hoped Clive wouldn't notice Faith Ann's dark brown curls and dark eyes that were so like his own.

"So, what does your husband do?"

"He's working in a lumber camp for this one year, and then he plans to go into business at the mill."

"Well, I'm working as a walker for the Waterhouse camps, and I get into Hitchcock every now and then. Maybe I'll see you around."

Katherine fastened Faith Ann's coat and moved toward the door. "Sure, come around anytime." She leaned on the door, opening it just a crack.

Clive stepped forward, pushed the door open wide, and followed Katherine outside. "See you later, Sam."

He stuffed his hands in his pockets, smiling down at her with eyes of pure delight.

"You've certainly become a handsome woman, Katherine. And your daughter's a real sweetheart." He gazed at Faith Ann, searching her face, her hair, her eyes. "And she looks just like her mother." Clive smiled and turned away.

"G'by, Mister Clive," Faith Ann called out. "I hope you can come to my house sometime."

"G'by, Faith Ann. Maybe I'll just do that; maybe I will." Katherine wasn't so sure that was a good idea; she didn't need any more complications in her life.

Later that afternoon, when Katherine and Hannah went to the hen house to gather eggs, Katherine broached the subject of Aunt Mae's overbearing personality.

"Hannah, you have to try harder to please your Aunt Mae. It wouldn't hurt you to fold the towels her way."

Hannah turned a surly look at Katherine. "Look who's talking! You don't like it any better than I do."

"I may not like it. And you may not like it. But as long as we're staying in Aunt Mae's home, we have to do things her way."

"Well, I'll be so glad if we ever get out of here! Why can't we fix up the Beasley house and move over there?"

"Hannah, you saw the living room at the Beasley's. It's in no condition for us to even think about."

"Well, the kitchen's OK. Why couldn't we board up the rest of the place and just live in the kitchen? We wouldn't be any more crowded there than we are here."

"And if we did move to the Beasley place, would you be happy? Your attitude toward me hasn't been exactly what you'd call warm and loving, you know."

Hannah's lips tightened into a thin line. "Well, what do you expect? You come intruding into my life. You take over my pa and drag us out into this wilderness. And I'm supposed to like it?"

Katherine had had it. She put down the basket of eggs and stared straight into Hannah's eyes. "Hannah, what is it with you, anyway? What have I done to make you dislike me so?"

Hannah's face transformed into a scowl. "Have you been around all this time and you don't know?" Her eyes tightened into little slits. "Well then, I'll tell you. First, you took my pa and you ignore me. It's Faith Ann this and Faith Ann that. I could leap over the moon and you'd never notice."

Katherine's heart beat a tattoo in her chest. "Is that so? Well, listen here, young lady. I've tried to make you feel good about us being a family. All you ever did was shove me away. You never listened to me, no matter what I said."

"Well, why should I listen to you? You're not my ma and you don't know anything about me."

"No, I'm not your ma. Your ma's dead just like mine. And it's no fun when your ma dies and leaves you alone. Night after night you cry in your pillow. You have this big, empty hole in your heart and no one can fill it, because it belongs only to her."

Hannah didn't answer and Katherine rushed on. "But at least you have a pa. I didn't have anyone."

Katherine grabbed her basket and headed toward the house. Hannah turned, pulling the chicken coop door shut and fastening it securely. Katherine and Hannah walked to the house in stinging silence.

That afternoon, Katherine thought about her argument with Hannah. Was it true? Did she really ignore Hannah and the good things the girl did? Had she noticed when Hannah helped Uncle Ned with the chores? She thought about the dishes Hannah washed and the meals she prepared and the beds she made. Maybe Katherine should try harder to show her appreciation. Could she make a friend of Hannah, now that they had aired their problem? Where should she go from here?

As the day wore on, Katherine thought about Hannah's suggestion that they move into the Beasley place. It really wasn't a bad idea. The kitchen was spacious and in good condition. Frank had thought Uncle Ned wouldn't have the money, but they'd never really asked. Was it possible that he could help, and they could make it happen? He and Aunt Mae might even be relieved to have their home to themselves again. As soon as Katherine got a chance, she'd talk to Uncle Ned.

That evening, Katherine found Uncle Ned sitting alone by the heater. His eyes were closed and his head nodding, but he seemed aware of her presence.

"Uncle Ned," she murmured.

Uncle Ned opened his eyes. "Hmmm?"

"I was talking to Hannah today, and she had an idea that might be worth thinking about."

"Yeesss?"

"Hannah was saying we could move into the Beasley place if we board up the doors and just use the kitchen area."

Uncle Ned made no move, and Katherine went on.

"I think it could work. The kitchen's in good shape and it's pretty good size. If we sealed the door between the kitchen and the rest of the house, we could move in. Then we could fix up the rest of the place, after Frank comes home in the spring. We could put a bed beside the door for me and one in the pantry for the girls. Then you and Aunt Mae could have your home to yourselves."

"Now, don't you worry none about us. We're just glad to do what we can to help."

"So what would be involved if we decided to move over there?"

Uncle Ned came fully awake. "Well, you'd have to pay five years' back taxes, probably somewhere around fifty dollars. But remember, the Beasleys would have three years to reclaim the place. And if they, did you'd lose all the hard work you'd put in."

A surge of energy filled Katherine's breast. Maybe she could make this thing work yet. "About those back taxes . . ."

She took a deep breath and broached the difficult proposition of finance. "I was wondering if you might be able to loan us the money. We could pay you when Frank comes back in the spring."

Uncle Ned's face fell. "I'm sorry, Katherine. I really would like to help, but there's just no way. We simply don't have the money."

Resignation flooded Katherine's being. "Thank you anyway," she said, rising from her chair. Then she turned toward the door.

"Well, now, hold on a minute." Uncle Ned rubbed his hand over his chin. "Actually, I think you could probably just go over there and move in."

"What?" Katherine slid back onto her seat. "You're saying we could move in without paying anything? Wouldn't that get us into a lot of trouble?"

"Who's going to stop you? The place is abandoned." A glimmer of hope crept back into Katherine's heart.

"I don't believe anyone hereabouts'll give two hoots if you're out there. If anyone complains, you just come back here, and Frank can pay those taxes when he gets the money."

Katherine smiled. Uncle Ned's reasoning made sense. And although he had denied it, Katherine wondered if the stress of living in close quarters was as difficult for him and Aunt Mae as it was for her and Hannah.

The next day Katherine stood at the kitchen range stirring a pot of rabbit stew, when the door burst open and Hannah entered.

"Hannah, if you've got a minute, I'd like to talk to you." Hannah stopped in her tracks, jaw tensed in stony opposition.

"What do you want?"

"Let's go to your room, where we can talk without being interrupted."

Hannah's eyes narrowed. "OK?"

She turned her back and walked resolutely into the pantry.

Taking a seat on Hannah's bed, Katherine motioned for Hannah to do the same, but Hannah stood unbending with eyes asquint. "Hannah, I think you'll be pleased with what I have to say. Why don't you sit down?"

Reluctantly, Hannah sat on the edge of the bed as far from Katherine as possible.

"Now, what do you want?"

"First of all, I want us to get along better. I'm going to try to pay more attention to the good things you do."

Hannah's eyes narrowed speculatively.

"And I've been considering your suggestion that we board up the dining room and move into the Beasley kitchen. I think it could work."

Hannah's eyes widened. "You do?"

"Uncle Ned says nobody would care, and if anyone says anything, we could move back here."

Katherine paused, waiting for her idea to take root. "And even if that happened, we'd be no worse off than we are now. Your pa could pay the taxes when he comes home."

"So why are you asking me? When have I ever made a difference?"

"Oh, Hannah, you do make a difference, especially now. We're in this situation together, and we have to make it work. It's important that we get along. If we move over there and then we get to bickering, it'll be miserable. Can you stand to live in one room and a pantry with me?"

Hannah took a deep breath and lowered her chin. She sat unmoving for a long while. "I'll try if you will," she said at last.

"That's all I ask."

Within days, Katherine and her family had moved into the Beasley house. There wasn't much to move—some clothing the family had bought since arriving in Hitchcock, and the beds, straw ticks, and bedding they'd been using at Uncle Ned's house. Hannah brought her case, and Faith Ann brought Ben, the old sock doll Aunt Mae had made to replace Annie.

Aunt Mae sent about twenty jars of canned goods from her cellar, and Uncle Ned brought a sled for Faith Ann.

"She can ride on it," he said. "And when you go to Hitchcock's, you can haul groceries and stuff on it."

Now if Katherine and Hannah could just get along, they'd be OK.

Chapter Ten

The next morning Katherine lay in her bed, mulling over the day's agenda. She'd sprinkled the clothes yesterday, and today she must iron. That would take the better part of the morning.

In the afternoon she hoped to work on the quilt she was making for Frank's homecoming. She'd designed it especially for Frank, with six red hearts of varying sizes, appliquéd on an off-white background and bordered with a double wedding-ring pattern. It would have two hearts entwined for Frank and her, and four smaller hearts of varying sizes for Seth, Hannah, Faith Ann, and Johnny. A soft place in Katherine's heart still reached out for a child that was no more.

But come spring, Frank would be home, and what remained of her family would be together forever. It was what she had wanted all her life—a secure, happy home with a husband and children, all living together as a unit. Katherine rose, started a fire in the range, and set the table for breakfast.

Soon the girls dashed out of their pantry bedroom. They huddled near the range, yanking on their clothing as fast as they could. Then Katherine served hot oatmeal, and she and her girls began their first morning in their new home.

By noon, Katherine had finished the ironing and set a batch of bread to rise. Hannah had taken care of morning chores, washing dishes, making beds, and such.

"Thank you, Hannah," Katherine said. "You've been a real help this morning."

A smile curled Hannah's lips as she opened her arithmetic book. "You're welcome, Katherine."

Katherine gathered the parts for Frank's quilt and spread them on the table. She threaded her needle and began the tedious job of sewing the little pieces of fabric together to form rings.

She considered her new relationship with Hannah. It did seem that things were getting better between them. As she worked, an old tune broke from her lips: "'Tis a happy day when the family's home."

"Frank, I'd like you to do rounds with me today."

Luc stood in the doorway, rubbing his hands together for warmth. "Emma has a big order coming in on the tote wagon, and Jasper wants to stay around to help store it."

Frank laid aside the camp books, threw on his mackinaw, and grabbed his scotch cap and mittens. He certainly wouldn't mind taking a break from the wanigan. He took one last look at the shelves stacked with wares and exited the store. Luc had hitched Blackie to the jumper, and soon they were headed for the woods, gliding along over the drifted snow.

When they stopped at the first worksite, Klause Bruner's chin flew upward and he snapped the reins.

"C'mon, you jackals," he yelled at the crew. "Show the boss what real he-men can do."

An extra burst of energy ignited the crew, and they flew into action. Horses labored up the cross-haul, a passageway that had been cut into the forest at right angles to the sleigh bunk. A fifteen-foot log rolled up the skids and onto the bunk where Boris Horowitz, the top loader, jostled it into place with his canthook. Log after log was hauled up the skids and onto the load. Until one log pitched forward.

"Where ya goin' ya wretched flip-up?" Craig Morris, the sender-up, flew into a flurry of unfit verbiage, as the large end of the trunk propelled itself upward and became misaligned to the bunk.

Craig caught the log with his canthook, hauling back on it, while Joe Dumont, the other sender-up, shoved hard on the lagging end. Both loggers spewed a litany of foul language, as if to scare the miscreant into submission. The timber groaned and fell into place.

When the layer was complete, the crew secured it with a toggle chain, and Hiram Breen tailed down the next log. The load grew, layer upon layer, until Boris stood five feet high on a pyramid of logs. The horses leaned into the harness, and the sleigh moved down the ice road to the landing, where the timber would await spring. Then the ice would thaw, and the winter's harvest would be herded down the river to the mill.

Frank admired Boris. It was dangerous business, dancing around atop a five or six-layer load of cantankerous logs. With each layer, the load grew higher and more dangerous. Many a toploader had been bashed to death when a load shifted and went crashing to the ground. But Boris did his job with real skill, and he had reason to be proud of his work.

It was early December and Katherine lay in her bed, reflecting on her good fortune to have moved into the Beasley house. Her new home had everything her family would need for the winter. To her right were the cupboards, a little brown with age, but when she finished decorating they would gleam in shining white. In the middle of the room stood the table with a red-and-white oilcloth she'd bought at Hitchcock's. And she'd fallen heir to a beautiful Hollister range with chrome trim and a large reservoir and warming oven. In the spring Frank would return. He'd renovate the rest of the place, and her family would live happily ever after.

In the pantry the girls slept soundly. Although there were still difficult times, Katherine's relationship with Hannah had improved a great deal. She lay quietly, listening to the stillness of the winter night, the crackling of the fire as it died down to a warm glow. A tide of peace settled upon her soul, and she closed her eyes, drifting happily off toward sleep.

Suddenly she was jarred into wakefulness. She thought she heard a noise in the woodshed.

She lifted herself onto her elbow, listening—straining. There it was again, a clunk and a scrape just outside the wall. Then the doorknob turned. Someone was trying to break into her home! Katherine lay still, terror paralyzing her muscles. She thought of her girls sleeping in the pantry, and realized she dared not run for safety.

Thump, thump, thump. The sound of footsteps thundered on the deck.

Katherine swung her legs over the side of the bed, preparing to defend her home. A loud crash echoed through the night. The door shuddered and creaked, as someone threw himself at it. The planks trembled in mortal combat with the hasp Uncle Ned had installed. *Bang, slam, thud.* The air was filled with profanity. Another crash and the door shivered on its hinges. An oath rang out and then a loud bellow. But the door held. Thank goodness for Uncle Ned's hasp!

Footsteps pounded down the steps, and the night grew still. Hardly daring to breathe, Katherine peeked out the window to see the silhouette of a man walking away from the porch. He was short, maybe five feet two inches, and thin and wiry. The man disappeared around the corner of the barn.

Katherine lay in her bed, trembling. The flannel sheet beneath her was soaked with sweat. What would she have done if that man had broken in? She was alone with two young girls to defend. She rose and tiptoed to the pantry door, peeking in to find her young ones sleeping soundly. What would she do if that man came back? It was well into the wee hours before Katherine fell asleep.

Hannah pushed her head out of the covers, drew in a breath of cold, winter air, and pulled the covers close around her shoulders, building courage to emerge into the frosty morning. Then she threw back the quilts, grabbed her clothes, and made a dash for the kitchen.

"Good morning, Hannah," Katherine said, as she spooned oatmeal into breakfast bowls. "Did you sleep well?"

Hannah hovered over the kitchen range, yanking her clothes over her cold body. "Morning," she said, scrambling into her underwear. She slipped her feet into a pair of long cotton stockings, wrapped the legs of her underwear tightly around her ankles, and eased the hose up over them, securing the stockings with a garter.

"I slept OK once I got to sleep. I kept thinking about Pa and how surprised he'll be when he finds out we're here."

Hannah filled the washbasin with warm water from the reservoir and splashed it onto her face. She wiped on a worn towel that hung near the washstand, ran a comb through her hair, and then folded it into a braid that hung half way down her back.

Soon, Faith Ann burst through the doorway. "It's c-c-cold," she said, shivering in her nightgown.

Hannah helped her little sister into her long underwear, pulled the child's stockings up over the legs, and helped her into a dress.

"Thank you for helping with Faith Ann," Katherine said. Hannah's breast swelled. "You're welcome," she responded. Hannah could tell that Katherine was trying to show more appreciation for the good things she did around the house, and it made her feel good.

"And don't forget," Katherine continued. "Faith Ann and I are going to Sam's for supplies this afternoon. We're planning to meet you there after school."

"I remember," Hannah said.

After breakfast, Hannah cut two slices of bread, spread one with a thick layer of butter and strawberry jam, and put the other slice on top. She wrapped the sandwich in a cloth and placed it in the old syrup pail she used as a lunch pail. She added an apple and a hard-boiled egg and clapped on the cover.

"I think I'll leave early today," she said. "I don't know how long it'll take to walk from here."

She pulled on her snow pants and fastened them at her waist, allowing her skirt to hang out so it wouldn't get wrinkled.

She donned her coat, hat, and boots, and then thrust her hands into her mittens, grabbed her lunch, and hurried out the door.

In the woodshed, Hannah paused. Something wasn't right. Faith Ann's sled lay upside down on the earthen part of the floor. She stepped around it and exited the house. Her brow furrowed in confusion as she noticed footsteps leading all the way from the house to the barn. Uncle Ned must have gone out there for something when he was here the last time, although Hannah didn't remember noticing the tracks before.

She paused only a moment and went on her way. Shivering, she pulled her coat close around her body, a defense against a blast of cold weather that had come up in the night. She turned her face away from the wind, walking backward down the snow-covered road toward Hitchcock.

As she walked, she thought about her life. She didn't seem to mind Katherine's oversight these days. Maybe it was because her pa was gone and she needed a friend. Maybe it was because Katherine was the nearest thing she had to a mother. Or maybe it was because of the problem she'd had with Aunt Mae. At least Katherine didn't try to control her every move.

Rounding the corner onto Main Street, Hannah turned into the wind, hunkered down, and ran toward school.

CHAPTER ELEVEN

Katherine sat at the table preparing a list for the trip to Hitchcock's. She didn't need milk or eggs or canned goods; Aunt Mae had provided them. Sugar, flour, salt . . .

Something moved outside her window. Silently she tiptoed across the room, remembering last night's visitor. Her heart pounded like a sledge in her chest. She peered outside at the fields, at the barn, at the road. She nearly jumped out of her shoes as a gust of wind pushed at the elm tree outside. And a branch lashed past the window. She'd seen nothing more than a tree limb flailing in the air.

Katherine, get a hold of yourself, she thought. *That man was probably just a wanderer, looking for a place to sleep.* On the other hand, he might have been a crook hiding from the law. What if he was a murderer and Katherine had unknowingly moved into his hideout? Should she tell the girls about him? Would it be dangerous for them not to know? Katherine didn't want to scare her girls for nothing, but neither did she want to expose them to danger. She dropped onto her bed, wavering in indecision.

Gradually, Katherine became aware of an intense quiet emanating from the pantry.

"Faith Ann," she called, "what are you doing?"

There was no answer. "Faith Ann?"

Still no answer.

Katherine tiptoed to the pantry door and peeked in to find Faith Ann sitting on the floor with her back turned. The contents of Hannah's case lay scattered across the floor in front of her.

"Faith Ann, what are you doing?"

Faith Ann jumped to her feet, holding something behind her back.

"Faith Ann?" Katherine's eyes narrowed and she reached out her hand. "Give it here."

Faith Ann looked up with frightened eyes and stood rigid. "Faith Ann?"

Slowly, Faith Ann drew the forbidden object forward and dropped it into Katherine's palm.

It was Grandmother Hamlin's brooch.

"Faith Ann McLean, what are you doing with Hannah's brooch?"

Faith Ann's eyes misted over. "I was just lookin' at it."

"If Hannah catches you with that brooch, she'll be hopping mad, and she'll have every right."

Katherine swatted Faith Ann's backside and scooted her out the pantry door. She picked up Hannah's things and tucked them back into the case, depositing the brooch safely between the towels. "Now you stay out here, where I can keep an eye on you."

"I didn't mean no trouble," Faith Ann cried. "I just wanted to look at Hannah's pin. It's a pretty pin, and I like it." She flopped onto Katherine's bed, sobbing as if her heart would break.

Katherine took a seat on the edge of the bed, lifted Faith Ann onto her lap, and wrapped her arms about her baby.

"I still love you," she whispered. "But you mustn't be messing with things in Hannah's case."

"I won't do it again, Mama. I promise."

Katherine held her little girl in her arms until the tears died away. Then she boosted Faith Ann onto the floor. "Now then, let's get ready to go see Mr. Sam."

Faith Ann grabbed her snowsuit from the nail on the wall and shoved a leg into the pants. "I like Mr. Sam; he gives me candy."

But try as she might, the little girl couldn't get the suit to hold still long enough to put the other leg through the opening.

"Here, let me help you," Katherine offered. "No, I'm a big girl. I can do it."

"Yes, you are a big girl, but snowsuits are hard."

Faith Ann pulled and tugged and tugged and pulled, trying to get into the pants, but the snowsuit fought her every effort. In the end the little girl turned to her mother. "It's a hard job," she whimpered.

So Katherine held the unwieldy garment, while Faith Ann stuffed the other leg into the snowsuit. Then Katherine donned her own coat and hat, pulled on her gloves, and opened the door.

As she stepped outside, her knees almost buckled under her. The tracks in the snow were still there, and the remembrance of that awful figure in the night brought unfathomable fear. She turned her back on the pain and headed for Hitchcock's, holding tightly to her little girl's hand.

"Sam," Katherine said as they entered the store, "can you set up an account for me? I'm going to need some supplies."

"Sure thing, Katherine. I've been wondering how long before you'd get around to that. By the way, I heard you're moving into the Beasley place."

"You heard right. We moved in two days ago. Uncle Ned sealed off the door to the dining room, and we're living in the kitchen. It's the only part of the place that's livable."

Katherine laid her list on the counter. "When Frank gets home, he can work on the rest of the building."

"So what're you hearing from Frank these days? Anything?"

"Not much. They don't give time off for letter writing, you know." Abruptly the door opened and Hannah entered the store.

"Hi, you guys, sorry I'm late, but we didn't get out on time. Miss Verena wants us to do a book report."

The young woman turned to Sam. "Mr. Hitchcock," do you have a copy of *Little Women*?

Sam pointed. "It's right over there. The books are shelved by author, so it'll be near this end under A for Alcott."

81

Hannah found the book, and Sam added it to Katherine's order. Then he turned back to Hannah.

"Did you know Miss Alcott has another one out? It's titled *Little Men.* I've ordered it in, and you'll likely want that one, too."

Sam packed the order, and Katherine and her family took their leave.

Outside, they stacked the groceries on the sled, and Katherine took Faith Ann by the hand. Then she and her girls made their way back to the Beasley place.

Frank stretched and rolled over. He could have stood another hour's sleep, but he threw back the covers and sat up. With no cookees, he and Jasper had been pressed into service in the kitchen. Throwing on his clothes, he headed toward the cook shanty in the darkness of early morning. He washed the red-checkered oilcloths on the two long tables, while Emma cooked pancakes and Jasper set out forty-two tin cups with plates and silverware.

Before long, Luc entered the cook shanty with the walker, a tall, lean man with brown hair that curled around his ears. They took their places at the head of the table, as Jasper stepped outside to beat on the triangle. Many camps used a long gabrel-horn to call the jacks to meals, but at DuBois the gabrel was not deemed necessary.

Soon the men entered and took their places on the benches that lined the tables. Everyone knew his place, as assigned by camp pecking order, and no one was allowed to deviate. The men filled their plates from the mountains of flapjacks, and soon the serving dishes were emptied.

"More morning glory down here," called a jack, and Jasper set a fresh platter of pancakes in front of him. The man slapped three of the cakes onto his plate, drowned them in molasses, and shoveled a bite into his mouth.

"Loggin' berries," called another jack, and Frank brought a bowl of prunes.

The only sound was that of heavy munching, as pancakes and sausage, baked beans, and fried potatoes evaporated into nothingness. The feasting continued for maybe fifteen minutes before the jacks rose abruptly and left the shanty without having uttered another word.

Then Luc and the walker, along with Jasper, Emma, and Frank, sat down to a more leisurely breakfast.

"Clive Isaman," Luc said, as the kitchen crew took their seats, "I'd like you to meet Frank, our new clerk. He and Jasper have been helping Emma in the kitchen."

Before Clive or Frank could respond, Jasper leaned forward demanding attention. "By the way, Luc, how long does this double duty stuff go on before you get us a cookee?"

Luc shook his head. "Not much longer, I hope. Goodness knows, I've been trying, but there just doesn't seem to be anybody out there. Anyone who's willing to spend the winter out here is a hewer or a swamper or something, and he doesn't want to lug water and do dishes and such like."

"Well, if you want to know the truth, Frank and I don't want those duties, either." Jasper shot a glance at Frank. "Do we, Frank?"

"Maybe we can find someone at Christmas time," Luc said, "while we're in town."

"Well, I sure hope so. I'm getting pretty sick and tired of all this messing around."

As the meal progressed, Jasper and Luc gave an overview of camp needs, Clive brought news of world events as reported in the Police Gazette.

Then Frank and Clive retired to the wanigan to go over the books.

In time, Clive pushed back his chair and rose to his feet. "OK, so let's go find Luc and Jasper and take a look at the camp."

Through the remainder of the day, Frank, Luc, Jasper, and Clive inspected the camp. They examined the ice roads with their deliberately formed ruts. It was those ruts that controlled the glide of the sleighs to the decking grounds. They watched the road monkeys, sanding the inclines to keep sleighs from overtaking the horses. They observed the sending-up and the tailing-down, noting the roll of the logs off the deck and onto the bunk.

Finally, about mid-afternoon they made their way back to the cook shanty, where the aroma of coffee and freshly baked bread wafted on the air. Emma filled their cups with "mornin' mud," brought a platter of cinnamon buns, and sat with them for an afternoon break.

That evening Frank lay in his bunk rereading his most recent letter from Katherine.

> *Dear Frank,*
>
> *I have news that I hope will please you. Hannah and Faith Ann and I have moved into the Beasley place. Your Uncle Ned boarded up the door between the kitchen and the rest of the house, and we're living in the two rooms that aren't wrecked. It was Hannah's idea.*
>
> *Uncle Ned said no one would care, and if anyone complains, we can move back with him.*
>
> *We're all OK. Sam has agreed to sell some of my baked goods from the store, so we have a little income, and that helps. He set up an account for us, and our needs are pretty much cared for.*
>
> *Hannah and I seem to have found a common meeting ground. I don't know how long it will last, but for now we're getting along quite well.*
>
> *Faith Ann remains as determined as ever to be a big girl. She tries to read Hannah's books, so I ordered a copy of McGuffy's reader from Sam, and Hannah is reading it with her. She's really quite smart and can even recognize some of the words.*
>
> *Missing you, as always,*
> *Katherine*

Frank laid the letter aside. It pleased him to know that his family was happy and getting on with life. As soon as possible he'd go into Boyne City and pay those taxes.

CHAPTER TWELVE

Clive lifted his chin to the breeze, breathing deeply as he walked along the DuBois Camp tote road. The sun sparkled off the snow-covered ground, warming his bones. Many of the walkers these days traveled by horse or on railroads, but Clive simply enjoyed his time in the woods. He relished the sound of the birds singing in the treetops and the gentle whisper of the breeze as it whiffled through the brush. He even enjoyed the snow and the images it formed along ridges and streams.

He passed the immense granite rock that marked the edge of the cuttings. North of the rock stood a deep, uncut forest. To the south lay a vast field of stumps where jacks had harvested lumber—stump-land it was called.

Turning onto a narrow, two-track lane, Clive headed for the Nilsson cabin, where he planned to eat lunch. Maggie Nilsson was always happy to provide a meal in return for a few hours' company. It must be a lonely existence for Maggie and her thirteen-year-old daughter, Willowbelle, left alone for weeks at a time, while husband and father, Max, was out tending his trap lines. But Maggie stayed—a stalwart support for the man she had married many years ago at age fourteen.

Looking up, Clive could see the cabin with Lulu, their cow, milling about in the yard. As he approached, Willowbelle came to meet him. Sabaka, her big, mongrel dog who appeared to be about half wolf, led the way.

Willowbelle fairly gushed with delight. "Mr. Clive, it's good to see you."

Clive reached out to stroke Sabaka's head, rubbing the fur between her ears and patting her neck. "I always look forward to stopping by, Willow. How are you doing?"

"OK, I guess. Just working the place 'n' tending the animals 'n' stuff." As Clive and Willowbelle walked toward the rough board building that was the Nilsson home, Maggie appeared in the doorway with her arms outstretched.

"Clive Isaman, it's good to see you. Come on in and take a load off your feet. We ain't had a visitor since the last time you were here."

Clive entered the stark little cabin with its rough-hewn furnishings: a table made out of four one-by-eight-inch boards and set on legs made out of two-by-fours, a board-backed bench with a cornhusk tick that served as a settee, and four three-legged stools for chairs. He dropped his coat in a corner, shoved aside several towels that had been tossed on the bench-sofa, and took a seat.

"It's always a good day when you stop by," Maggie said, wiping her hands on her apron.

Clive rested his hand on the pile of towels. "And I keep coming back because you make me feel so welcome."

He looked across the room at three potato crates stacked on their sides and open in front to form shelves for Willowbelle's books. Those books were the one extravagance these women allowed themselves.

"So, Maggie, how are things?"

Maggie brushed a wisp of gray hair from her too-thin face. "Things are as always, I guess. Nothing much changes out here." Clive smiled. Maggie was a good woman, honest and dependable. She always took things in stride.

"I got coffee and a pot o' mulligan stew out here that's just lookin' for someone who needs a good meal. How 'bout if you help us with it?"

"That'd be nice, Maggie."

Maggie headed for the kitchen. "Willow, you set the table while I dish up the stew."

As Willow reached toward a high shelf for the cups and bowls, Clive noticed her long, lean arms, still brown from last summer's sun. *Like mother like daughter,* he thought. Both were tall and thin, downright skinny.

"Come and get it," Maggie called, and Clive joined the Nilssons to share a fine meal of vegetable stew with thick slabs of bread and freshly churned butter. For dessert, Maggie had opened a jar of huckleberries and served them with a generous layer of thick, rich cream and a sprinkling of sugar. Maggie knew huckleberries were one of Clive's favorites, and she served them nearly every time he came by.

"Maggie, I'm on my way to Hitchcock," Clive announced as he ate. "And I'll be coming back this way. Is there anything I can get for you while I'm there?"

"Not really, Clive. We get along pretty good out here by ourselves. We have lots of canned goods from last summer's garden, and we get the wild berries and things as they come ripe. We got chickens for eggs and Lulu for milk. About the only things we need from town are sugar and coffee and things, and Max brings a good supply of those when he comes."

"And how is Max? Is there enough game out there to keep things together for you folks?"

"We get by. Max has his trap lines strung out from here to eternity. He comes in when he can, but he's gone a lot, too. When he shows up, he's always OK, and he has the stuff we need from town. As for keeping things together, Willow 'n' I get along fairly well by ourselves."

"You ever think about moving into town?"

"Oh, yes, sometimes it seems like a good idea, but we never quite get around to it. Willow's got her books, you know, and she reads to me. She can read real good. Sister Olivia teaches her sometimes when she comes to the camps with them hospital cards. Most of the time we're working our tails off, anyway. We've always got canning or gardening or hauling wood or something to do."

"Speaking of hauling wood, Maggie, how about if I bring in a supply before I leave?" Clive knew what Maggie's answer would be, but it seemed appropriate to offer.

"Not today, Clive. The wood box is full. We'd rather you just sit here and visit for a spell."

So Clive sat on the bench and discussed the weather and the lumber camps and the fire that had burned the little village of Higgins nearly to the ground. And, of course, he brought the latest news from the *Police Gazette*. After a couple of hours, he reached for his pack.

"Well folks, I guess I'd better be on my way. I'm not going to get anything done if I sit around all day."

Disappointment flashed across Maggie's countenance, but she pasted on a smile and saw him to the door.

"It was good to see you, Clive. Be sure to stop again the next time you come by."

"I will, Maggie. I will."

Willow grabbed her coat. "Ma, I'm going to walk Mr. Clive down the lane."

"All right, but get yourself right back here. We have to cure those hides your pa brought in last week."

Clive and Willow left the cabin, strolling leisurely down the lane while discussing Willow's life in the woods and her pa and the trap lines.

"Mr. Clive," Willow said at last, "I've been wondering what it'd be like if we lived in town and I went to school. Do you think I'm smart enough to go to school? Maybe I could learn to be a midwife or something . . . if we lived in town, I mean."

"I'm sure you could do it, Willow. You're a smart young lady, and you could be a midwife or most anything you chose."

Willow's eyes grew pensive. "Maybe . . . maybe someday."

They reached the end of the lane, and Willow looked up at Clive with sadness in her eyes. But she, like her mother, left him with a smile.

"Goodbye, Mr. Clive. It was good to see you. Maybe my pa'll be home next time you stop." Willow said the words, but both she and Clive realized it wasn't likely.

"Willowbelle, how about if I buy a book for you while I'm in town? Would you like that?"

"I'd like that, Mr. Clive. I'd like that a lot."

"I know you have *Little Women*. I'll see if I can get *Little Men* for you."

"That would be really nice, Mr. Clive. Ma and I have read *Little Women* most a dozen times or so."

"I'll see what I can do."

Clive bade Willow goodbye and went his way with a spring in his step. He threw back his shoulders, chanting as he walked. "You're welcome every evening in Maggie Murphy's home."

Two hours later, Clive entered Hitchcock's General Store. "Sam, do you remember the last time I was here? There was a woman named Katherine in the store. She was an old friend of mine, and we hadn't seen each other since we were young. She had a little girl with her—do you remember?"

"You mean Katherine McLean. The family just moved to the area this year. They're kin of Ned McLean."

Clive's brow furrowed. "McLean. I just came from the Luc DuBois camp. His straw boss is named McLean, Jasper McLean. And there's a clerk named Frank McLean. She wouldn't be related to Jasper and Frank would she?"

"Yep, Frank's her husband. They came here to work in the camp with Jasper."

"Well, how do you like that? I just spent a whole day looking over the DuBois camp with Frank McLean."

"I'm told he's going to set up a milling shop here in town come spring."

"So where do they live? I'd like to look them up."

"Try the Beasley place." Sam nodded his head toward the north. "Katherine and the girls moved out there a week or so ago."

"The Beasley place, huh?"

"Don't go to the front door, though. They're only using the kitchen. The rest of the place's too badly torn up."

"Thanks, Sam."

Clive turned, sprinted off the front porch, and strode down the road toward Birch Lake.

Fifteen minutes later he stood at the back door entry to Katherine's home. As he waited for her to answer his knock, he kicked idly at a chunk of wood that lay nearby. Thunk—it flew into a homemade, wooden sled and fell to the earthen floor. He continued to knock, but the only response was silence.

You don't suppose any of them could be in the barn, he wondered. *Probably not, but I'll take a run out there just the same. At the very least it'll fill some time and maybe they'll return while I'm here.*

Clive made his way to the barn, leaving a path in the snow. But the barn was deserted. The only sign of life was a pile of hay that had been thrown down from the haymow overhead. It looked as if someone had slept there recently, and he wondered who it might have been. Disappointed, Clive went on his way.

Sleigh bells jingled in the early dusk as Katherine and her family glided along, snug and warm under Aunt Mae's quilt. A week or so ago, Hannah had suggested a surprise birthday party for Aunt Mae, and she had been planning the event ever since. Katherine made a cake, and Hannah decorated it with the words Happy Birthday, Aunt Mae across the top and with red roses on white icing around the edge. Hannah's roses were less than perfect, but they were a bright accent on the cake, and Aunt Mae didn't seem to notice their inexact form.

It had been a fine day, and Katherine was proud of her teenaged stepdaughter. "You did a good thing today, Hannah," she said.

"Thank you," Hannah responded. "And thanks for your help."

A sudden burst of tenderness enveloped Katherine, and she awakened to the realization that her bond with Hannah was becoming substantial. Without stopping to consider her action, she patted her stepdaughter on the knee.

Hannah's eyes widened in surprise and then, just as quickly, her face melted into a grin. She leaned toward Katherine and whispered. "It was fun wasn't it?"

Before Katherine could respond, Uncle Ned called from the driver's seat, "Shall we stop at Hitchcock's on the way?"

"No, thank you," Katherine answered.

The little group passed through the village without a pause, observing Christmas decorations everywhere. There were candles in the church windows and a wreath on the front door. A sign had been placed in the front yard: *Unto You a Child is Born; Merry Christmas.*

A tree stood at the Grange Hall, covered with sprigs of holly and apples and black walnuts. Sam's store was resplendent with acorns and holly berries and chestnuts. Hans Kubek had placed an old sleigh in front of his shop with two stuffed figures sitting in the seat. *Christmas Greetings from the Kubeks,* read the sign by its side. Faith Ann squealed and pointed with excitement.

Soon the sleigh turned into Katherine's yard, and she and the girls climbed onto the ground.

"We'll be OK," Katherine called. "You get on back to Aunt Mae. It's still her birthday, you know. And tell her we had a great time."

"Thank you, I will."

Uncle Ned flicked the reins and the sleigh moved down the road, leaving Katherine and her girls standing in the drive.

"Bring an armload of wood when you come inside, will you, Hannah?" Katherine asked as they turned toward the back door. "The wood box is about empty."

"I c'n get some wood too," Faith Ann said. "I'm a big girl."

"You sure can," Hannah responded. She took Faith Ann by the hand, and the two girls ran toward the woodshed.

Moments later, Katherine rounded the back corner of the house, and a wall of terror cascaded over her body. There were fresh tracks in the snow, marking a path from the house to the barn.

Katherine froze. She could still hear that man banging on the door, throwing himself against it, and stomping down the porch steps. Who was he, and what did he want? Why did he hang around? Was he out there right now?

"Let's get just enough wood for tonight." Katherine spoke slowly and deliberately, trying to hide the fear that permeated her bones. She stooped and filled her arms with wood.

When Katherine's family was safe inside, she locked and bolted the door, preparing to talk to her girls.

"Hannah," she said, "you light the lamps, while I build a fire." Soon the fire's warmth radiated throughout the room, and Katherine called to her girls.

"Hannah, Faith Ann, come here. I have something to tell you."

She boosted Faith Ann onto her lap and motioned for Hannah to take a seat. "Girls, did you notice a path outside in the snow, the one that led from the house to the barn?"

"Yes," Hannah said. "I saw it the other morning, too. I thought Uncle Ned must have been out there or something."

"Uncle Ned c'n walk real good in the snow," Faith Ann said. "I think he could make that path."

"Uncle Ned didn't make that path." Katherine paused to emphasize the seriousness of what she was about to say. "There was a strange man out there the other night. I don't know who he was or where he came from. Probably he just walked across our yard on his way to the woods, but I want you to be careful. Faith Ann, don't go outside alone. And Hannah, keep your eyes peeled for anything that shouldn't be out there. And don't hang around outside any more than you have to."

Faith Ann's eyes grew big as saucers. "Mama, do we got a bad man at our house?"

"I wouldn't say that. I just don't want you to take any chances, that's all."

Hannah's gaze leaped to the bolt on the door. "And we'd better keep the door locked."

"Yes, but let's not get so scared we can't enjoy our home." Katherine stood Faith Ann on the floor. "Now then, why don't you girls get ready for bed, while I do the ironing?"

She patted Faith Ann on the back and set up the ironing board, hoping the girls couldn't hear her knees knocking together.

Hannah brought the girls' nightgowns from the pantry, and they changed clothes near the range. Then they dashed into their pantry bedroom, where they would snuggle together for warmth and fall asleep as their bodies warmed the air under the heavy quilt.

CHAPTER THIRTEEN

Hannah's heart sang as she set the table for supper. Next week her pa was coming home, and the McLeans had spent the whole day getting ready for the big celebration at Uncle Ned's house. Hannah and Uncle Ned had cut the most beautiful Christmas tree ever and set it up in the sitting room. Aunt Mae said it was too big and had a hollow spot on one side, but they placed the hollow part against the wall, and Hannah didn't think the tree was too big at all.

Katherine had made a dishpan full of popcorn and dyed half of the kernels red with beet juice dye. Then she and Hannah strung them in long red-and-white strands, draping them in loops and swirls around the tree. There were no candles; Aunt Mae said it was too easy for trees to catch fire when you put candles on them.

There would be a big Christmas dinner with ham and mashed potatoes and gravy and cranberry sauce and all the trimmings. Hannah baked a pumpkin pie and Katherine made sweet rolls and sugar cookies. Faith Ann smeared icing on some of the cookies . . . and all over the table while she was at it.

Uncle Ned shelled a syrup pail full of black walnuts. He always said there was nothing like black walnuts for eating, but getting 'em out of the shells was like pryin' the truth from a blue-faced liar.

And Pa would be home for the school program at the Grange Hall. Hannah was really looking forward to it, for she was to give the welcoming speech and sing with the chorus. Then, after the program, she would stand at the door with the older kids and hand out candy. The world was a beautiful place. Hannah's pa was coming home.

Katherine's hands flew over the quilt top she was making for Frank's homecoming. She planned to show him the partly finished work while he was home for the Christmas holidays. Beside her on the floor sat two evergreen branches, tied together, and held upright in a wooden holder. They were to be the McLeans' Christmas tree.

At the moment, Hannah and Faith Ann were out in the woodshed, fussing over a couple of potato crates they planned to put under the branches. Faith Ann had apparently decided she could carry one of them, and Hannah disagreed. Hannah's voice came ringing through the wall.

"Faith Ann, you'll never get it over the doorsill."

"I can do it," came the response. "I'm a big girl."

"You girls quit your arguing," Katherine called.

The door flew open, and Hannah entered carrying a crate. "OK, you just try!"

Faith Ann came behind her sister, struggling to get the crate up the step and over the threshold.

"I told you that you couldn't do it," Hannah snapped. "But you wouldn't listen."

Tears of frustration pooled in Faith Ann's eyes. "I c'n do it," she stammered. She struggled in a valiant tug of war with the unruly crate, but it seemed to have a mind of its own.

Finally Katherine lifted the crate over the doorsill, and Faith Ann dragged the troublesome box inside.

"I did it, Hannah," she countered. "I'm a big girl."

Hannah just rolled her eyes and went about her business. She set the two crates atop one another in front of the dining room door. Then she covered them with a sheet and lifted the Christmas branches, placing them carefully so they spread as wide as possible.

"OK, Faith Ann, hand me that chain," she said.

Faith Ann held out the paper chain the girls had made from colored pages of the *Michigan Farmer* magazine.

"Here, you hold this end," Hannah said, "while I put it in place."

Together the girls managed to drape the garland over the branches. "Now get those paper cubes I folded the other day," Hannah said.

Faith Ann took off on the run into the pantry, returning shortly with a shoebox. "Here they are," she called.

Soon the branches were finely adorned with a paper chain, paper-cube ornaments, and a paper star that Katherine placed at the very top.

"Merry Christmas, girls," she said. "I'm sure your pa will love it." Frank would be returning that evening and Katherine could hardly wait.

Early in the evening, the door flew open and Frank stepped inside.

"Merry Christmas," he called. "What's for supper?"

"Pa's home," Hannah yelled. She threw herself at Frank's torso, as Faith Ann assaulted his legs.

"Hold on there, girls," Frank blurted. "You 'bout knocked me over." He laughed and hugged his girls, lifting Faith Ann into his arms and tickling her under the chin.

"I was a big girl," Faith Ann said. "I helped trim the Christmas tree."

Frank laughed, put Faith Ann onto the floor, and pulled Hannah into a warm hug. Then he held his daughter at arm's length, gazing into her eyes with paternal love.

"Hannah," he said, "you're my big girl, a capable young woman, and it's great to see you."

Hannah's eyes brimmed with joy. "Oh Pa," she cried, "it's so good to have you home. I thought you'd never get here."

Finally, Frank moved near to Katherine with eyes full of devotion. He put his arms around her waist and held her close for a long minute. "I've missed you," he whispered.

"And I've missed you." Katherine laid her face on her husband's chest; her heart warmed with satisfaction.

After a moment, Frank stepped back and took in his surroundings. "And look at this new house you ladies have. You've certainly been busy while I was gone."

"It was my idea," Hannah quipped. "We got to come here because I suggested it."

Katherine smiled. "That's right; it was Hannah's idea . . . and a good one, too."

"I helped Hannah make a Christmas tree," Faith Ann chimed in.

Katherine smiled and removed a pan from the warming oven.

"Anybody ready for supper?"

"Mmm, chicken pot pie," Frank said, taking a seat at the table as Hannah placed plates and silverware for everyone.

For Katherine it was a joyful time, just sitting beside her husband in their new home.

Soon supper was finished and Katherine pushed back her chair. "OK, girls," she said. "It's time to go."

Hannah leaped to her feet, rushed into the pantry, and emerged resplendent in her Sunday dress.

"That's my beautiful daughter," Frank said, and he held out Hannah's coat as if to honor a grand lady.

Then the McLean family left the house on foot, walking toward the Grange Hall and the school program. There, Hannah disappeared behind a curtain stretched across the entire front of the building. Katherine and Frank ambled toward the front seats with Faith Ann and found places beside Uncle Ned and Aunt Mae. Jasper and Emma arrived shortly thereafter, taking seats nearby in the next row. All the while, Faith Ann clung to her pa like paste.

It was an exciting time, and the community was charged with anticipation.

Finally, the clock on the wall struck seven and Hannah appeared before the crowd. She looked right at Frank with eyes that shouted her joy.

"Welcome to our Christmas program," she said. "Tonight is a very special night. We have spent many hours learning our parts, preparing scenery, and decorating the hall. But the time has been well spent and we are excited to celebrate the

Christmas holidays with you. Now, please sit back, relax, and enjoy our presentation."

The curtain opened to reveal the entire student body standing on risers built by Horace Brace several years before. After the celebration, the risers would be returned to Horace's barn until spring, when they would be brought back and set up for the Easter program.

Miss Verena took her place at the piano, and Hannah stepped into the back row.

And the strains of Christmas filled the room. There were carols, recitations and skits. Then Cliff Britt came forward to read the Christmas story from the second chapter of Luke. As he took his seat, the entire student body called out their joy. "Merry Christmas!" they shouted, "and Happy New Year!"

At the door, Hannah handed Faith Ann a Christmas box with ribbons and bells and holly printed on its sides.

"Look what I got," the little girl cried as the family climbed into Uncle Ned's sleigh. "Hannah said it's candy."

"Sure enough," Frank responded. "I believe it's candy."

Uncle Ned flicked the reins, and the horses trotted off toward the Beasley place.

Hannah's heart was so filled with excitement that she began to sing, "Jingle bells, jingle bells, jingle all the way." The family joined in, filling the night air with holiday joy. Almost too soon, the ride was over and Uncle Ned bade the McLeans goodnight. He urged the horses on, leaving Katherine and her family at their door.

The next morning, as Katherine stood before the range making pancakes, Frank slipped up behind her.

"Merry Christmas," he whispered. "How are you doing this morning, Mrs. McLean?"

Katherine leaned against his chest. "I'm happier than I've been in weeks."

She stood in the circle of Frank's arms for several minutes until the girls entered and the room was filled with chatter.

Katherine poured oatmeal into the bowls, and the family took their places at the table for breakfast.

It was barely eight o'clock when the McLeans gathered around the Christmas branches for gift giving. Katherine selected a package wrapped in tissue paper and tied with green-and-red Christmas cord.

"To Faith Ann, from Hannah," she read.

Everyone watched as the little girl pulled back the paper.

"It's a scarf and mittens," Faith Ann cried. She pulled on the mittens and wrapped the scarf around her shoulders.

Katherine reached out and touched Faith Ann's arm. "What do you say?"

"Thank you, Hannah." The little girl brushed the mittens over her face, feeling the soft yarn on her cheeks.

"I knitted them myself," Hannah said.

Next, Katherine selected a flat package wrapped in green Christmas paper.

"To Hannah, from Katherine," she read.

Hannah's eyes grew tender, and she looked at Katherine with a warm regard that blessed Katherine's heart. The young woman untied the bow and pulled back the wrapping, taking care not to tear the paper lest it become unusable for next year's gifts.

"Pillowcases for my hope chest," she murmured. She ran her fingers over the multicolored flowers embroidered on the ends. "They're very pretty, thank you."

"And here's one for Faith Ann from your pa and me."

Katherine handed a box to the little girl, and Faith Ann opened it as carefully as her sister had.

"Oh, clothes for Ben," she hollered. She ran into the pantry after the doll.

"And the ribbon is for you to wear in your hair," Katherine called.

Next, Frank selected a small box about the size of a matchbox for Hannah. Inside, Hannah found a decorative comb for her hair—a beautiful comb with a tortoise shell back and a row of six shiny rhinestones.

"I bought it in Boyne City," he said.

Hannah pushed the comb into her hair, preening like a peacock. "Thank you, Pa."

Soon it was time for Frank's gift, and Katherine picked a brown paper bag from the crates under the branches. "This one's for you, Frank," she said. "It's not finished, but I wanted you to see it."

She pulled out the center piece for the gift and held it up. "It's to be a quilt," she said, "designed especially for your homecoming in the spring. The six hearts in the middle are for our family, one heart for each of us here, and one for Seth, and one for Johnny. And it'll have a double wedding-ring pattern around the edge for our union."

"Thank you, Katherine," Frank whispered. "That will be a grand way to mark a new beginning in our new home."

He turned toward the window, as if deeply interested in something outside. When he looked back, his eyes seemed damp.

Katherine returned the quilt pieces to the sack, and Frank reached into his pocket. He pulled out an envelope and handed it to his wife. "And this is my gift to you."

Katherine opened the envelope, and her eyes filled with tears. It was the gift of all gifts, a receipt for the taxes on their house.

"We have a home," she murmured. "And it is our very own." Near eleven o'clock, Katherine and her family set out for Christmas dinner at Uncle Ned's place, arriving just in time to find Aunt Mae pulling the ham out of the oven. She had cooked the potatoes and vegetables to perfection, making sure they were still hot when the ham was ready. She had spread the table with a fine white cloth and taken care to see that each plate was in place and the silverware properly positioned. When Aunt Mae was in charge, nothing was missed and everything ran smoothly. "As slick as oil," Uncle Ned said.

After dinner, Jasper and Frank spent much time discussing upcoming months at the lumber camp. Katherine and Emma built a new friendship, and Uncle Ned just hung in.

Faith Ann and Hannah played outside a good deal of the day. Then, about mid-afternoon, when the sun was its warmest, Frank and Jasper took the girls sledding on Parson's Dome. It was a fine trip, and the girls would chatter about the experience for the next week.

In time, the light dissipated from the sky, Aunt Mae lit the lamps, and everyone prepared to return home. Jasper invited Frank and the family to ride in his sleigh, and Katherine was more than happy to accept.

Over the next several days, Frank worked on the house. He closed the hole in the front room so the animals couldn't get in. He covered the broken window with a board, shored up the floors, and picked up the debris that cluttered the living room. The time had flown by, and now Frank must return to camp for the remainder of the long, hard winter. But first, Uncle Ned's tools must be returned.

"Katherine," he called. "Are you about ready?"

"I'm coming."

Katherine and the girls stepped out the door, bundled and ready for the walk. "Let's stop at Hitchcock's and pick up the mail," Katherine suggested. "And if there's anything for Uncle Ned, we can take it with us."

"Sounds good to me," Frank responded.

The McLeans walked easily down the road toward Hitchcock's General Store.

"Morning Sam," Frank called as they stepped inside. "How're things?"

"Good with me. And you?"

"We're on our way to Uncle Ned's. You got any mail for us?" Sam thumbed through a handful of envelopes. "Well let's see.

Here's a letter for your Uncle Ned. Comes from Canada; looks like something official."

He handed the letter to Frank. "And here's one for you from Boyne City." He held up an envelope, examining it both front and back. "What could the county be wanting of you?"

"I'm sure I don't know," Frank said.

"Well, I guess that's all." Sam stuffed the remaining letters back in the community box.

Frank took his letter, stepped out the door, and ripped it open. His eyes scanned the page and his face dropped.

> *To Mr. and Mrs. Frank McLean,*
> *From Harry Banks: County Treasurer*
>
> *Dear Mr. and Mrs. McLean,*
> *Enclosed please find a voucher for thirty-five dollars, per your payment on the taxes at 2110 Birch Lake Road in Hitchcock Michigan. The previous owner, Mrs. Richard Beasley, has reclaimed the property. Back taxes have been paid in full, and you must vacate the property within thirty days.*
>
> *Yours sincerely,*
> *Ann Mason: asst. county treasurer*
>
> *Enclosure: Voucher for thirty-five dollars.*

Frank handed the letter to Katherine, aching inside for the pain he knew it would bring.

As Katherine's eyes scanned the letter, he could feel her heart break. A home was the one thing she had desired most in life. Now, just as she was settling into her new place, it had been torn from her, like so many times before.

"What did the letter say, Pa?" Hannah wanted to know. "Oh, nothing you need to worry about."

Frank knew it was a lie, but the news would ruin the day for his girls. He walked toward Uncle Ned's house in silence. Of course, he'd have to tell Uncle Ned. How would he ever find the words?

CHAPTER FOURTEEN

Frank stood in the tool shed, watching as Uncle Ned punched a hole in the straps of Gretchen's harness.

"You seem awfully quiet today, Frank."

Frank braced himself, preparing for the moment of truth. "We got a letter in the mail today." He hesitated not wanting to go on.

"Well, spit it out, son. We can't deal with a problem 'til we know what it is."

"The Beasley house has been reclaimed."

Uncle Ned's shoulders dropped. He put aside the hammer and looked into Frank's eyes with obvious concern. "I'm really sorry to hear that, Frank, but you know all it means is that your family will need to move back here. We knew from the beginning that this could happen."

He placed a rivet through the holes and struck it lightly with a mallet.

"Yes, I realize that, and we appreciate it more than you know, but we really need a home of our own."

The door opened then, and Jasper came sauntering into the shed. "Ma said you two were out here. What's going on?"

Uncle Ned held up the harness, examining the rivet carefully. "Nothing much, just standing around talking."

"Well, there's something going on in the house. The women shut up like a bunch of clams, as soon as I walked in the room. Katherine looks like she just lost the last friend she ever had."

Frank steeled himself and turned toward Jasper. "I guess you might as well know. The Beasleys have reclaimed the house."

Jasper's brow furrowed. "So, what are you going to do now?"

"Move back here, I suppose. But the fact is this house is too small for two families."

Uncle Ned placed the harness on a nail and turned toward the door. "Just the same, you're always welcome. "Now c'mon inside. It's cold out here."

As they entered the house, Emma moved to Jasper's side. "Well, did Frank tell you?"

"Tell me what?"

"The Beasleys took the house back."

"Yes, he told me, and it's a rotten shame."

"Well, I have an idea." Emma looked from Katherine to Frank and then back to Jasper. "Why can't Katherine and Hannah come to the camp as cookees? They could live in the wanigan with Frank and get paid for staying there. And we'd have the help we need. Everybody wins."

Frank stood dumbfounded. "And what's Luc going to say when we come bringing a woman and two kids into camp?"

A conspiratorial smile spread across Emma's face. "I don't know, but it's worth a try. I'm a woman and I get along OK."

"Yes, but you're the cook."

"And Katherine and Hannah would be the cook's helpers. At the very worst, Luc wouldn't agree to the idea, and they'd have to come back here. And if that happens, they're no worse off than they are now."

Jasper's brow furrowed. "Well, it might work at that."

"Such a thought never entered my mind," Frank said. "What do you think, Katherine?"

Katherine's face was a study of incredulity. "Well, give us some time to think on it."

By the end of the day, the decision was made, and the McLeans prepared to move. Hannah gathered her schoolbooks along with her case containing Grandma Hamlin's brooch. Katherine collected the pieces for Frank's homecoming quilt so she could work on it over the winter. Faith Ann grabbed Ben and his new Christmas suit. The rest of their personal belongings would be stored in Uncle Ned's barn.

Katherine followed Emma into the cook shanty.

"This is the dining room," Emma said, holding out her arm. Two long tables stood the full length of the room, covered with red checked oilcloths. "You'll need to be here well before meal time. You'll stand over the tables to see that serving dishes are filled. You'll carry water and do dishes and such. In short you'll . . ."

Just then the door flew open, and a man about seven feet tall, with a chest as big as a bull, entered.

Katherine knew in a moment it must be Luc DuBois, the camp boss. With him came a heavyset man with a potbelly and a bald head.

"I got you a cookee, Emma. Angus Muldoon has agreed to tote for you."

The man's gaze fell on Katherine, and he recoiled in obvious disbelief.

"Emma, who is this?"

"Well, Luc." Emma pulled herself to full height, looking up at the man with an "I dare you" face. "It seems we both brought back cookees. This is Frank's wife, Katherine, my cousin. And this is their daughter, Hannah. And unless you've got someone else to cook for you, you'll treat them kindly."

Just then, Faith Ann came running from behind the counter. "And who is that?" The man's bellow nearly blew the roof off.

"That's Katherine's daughter. Her name is Faith Ann."

Luc's face grew calm, but his voice remained rock hard. "Well, they'll have to go back. We ain't got no place for a baby in this camp."

"I'm not a baby, mister. I'm a big girl."

The man just turned his back and stomped out the door.

Katherine took Faith Ann by the hand and walked across the road to the wanigan. "Frank, I just met Luc DuBois."

"And how did he react?"

"Well, he's not happy, to say the least." "I was afraid of that. What did he say?"

Katherine reached for her bag, her insides churning. "He just roared like a bull and left."

She looked around the wanigan at the stark furnishings. *Well, this place wasn't so hot anyway.*

Soon Luc entered the store. His jaw was a monolith set in stone. "Frank," he said, "I want to talk to you."

Without a word, Frank followed Luc through the office door and into the boss's quarters.

Katherine gritted her teeth and muttered a verbal beating under her breath. "Just what makes you think you're so special, anyway?" Her lips tightened into a sneer. "You're nothing but a big bull that has to have its own way." Katherine didn't want to hang around that hunk of trash, anyway.

It wasn't long until Frank returned, somber-faced and weary. "Luc says you can stay until the tote wagon comes, and then you'll have to go. You'll sleep here with me, and in the meantime, if Emma wants you to work in the kitchen, that's her business."

Katherine looked around the place. The merchandise area was on the left, separated from the living space by a counter and a locked gate. A small heater stood on the right with a couple of straight-backed chairs. There were two bunks at the far end of the room. The girls could sleep on the top, and she and Frank would use the bottom. Living space was small but livable. At least her family would be together for these few days.

Katherine later heard that Luc stomped into the bunkhouse about nine o'clock that night. He stood tall and menacing for several seconds and then let out a roar that might have knocked down an elephant, had one been in his way.

"I'm the toughest man around, and I can lick anyone in this bunkhouse." He glowered at the men one at a time.

No one moved or said a word. And Luc walked out.

The next day, Katherine and Hannah joined Emma in the cook shanty. They helped serve meals with Angus Muldoon; they carried water, cleared tables, and washed dishes. Katherine baked a batch of caramel cinnamon rolls that Luc appeared to think were about as good as any he'd ever eaten. Faith Ann sat on a bunk in a corner, playing with Ben and his new clothes.

It soon became apparent that word was out about a child in the camp. One by one the jacks came into the wanigan, looked around, and if Faith Ann weren't in the room, they walked out. If Faith Ann were nearby, they'd step up to the desk and order something.

"Gimme a bag o' Peerless," they might say or, "What-a-ya got fer a cold?"

While Frank or Katherine looked up the desired item, they'd turn to Faith Ann. "Well, hello young lady. What's your name?"

"I'm Faith Ann, mister, and this is my mama. We get to stay here in the woods with my pa for a little while. Maybe I'll be a lumberjack when I grow up."

The jack would laugh, pat Faith Ann on the head and introduce himself. "Well, I'm Bjorn Funk, and I got a little niece (or daughter, or sister) about your age."

And those rough-cut he-men melted. Soon Faith Ann was the mascot of the camp.

Several weeks had passed and the tote wagon came and went. Katherine and the girls remained at camp, with Hannah serving in the cook shanty with Angus Muldoon. Katherine spent most of her time helping Frank in the wanigan. She'd sent a request for cloth to hang a curtain in front of the bunks for privacy, and when she wasn't behind the counter or gathering requisitions from the in camp crew, she worked on the wedding-ring quilt. Frank had become increasingly involved with other activities, and today he had gone to Rifkin with Jasper to pick up a special order for Luc. Katherine had taken advantage of the moment to sew the rings for Frank's quilt.

Suddenly the door flew open and Luc pushed his way inside, ducking his head as always to avoid slamming it on the casing.

"Katherine, I'd like you to meet the walker."

Katherine looked up and nearly dropped Frank's quilt onto the floor. Before her stood Clive Isaman. He was tall and lean and as good looking as ever, with his Nordic face, rugged torso, and his cocoa brown hair curling around his ears.

Clive's eyes were saucers. "Katherine? I don't believe it. How did you get out here?"

He turned. "Luc, this is my childhood sweetheart." Faith Ann edged her way to her mother's side.

"Clive, this is my daughter, Faith Ann," Katherine said. "You met her at the store in Hitchcock. Do you remember?"

"Yes, I remember. How could I forget such a delightful little girl? How're you doing, young woman?" Clive's dark eyes sparkled, reminding Katherine of that day so long ago when she spilled lemonade on him, and he asked her for their first date. It was the beginning of their relationship and her first love. What would he think if he knew this child was his daughter? No, he must never learn.

"Clive I . . ."

But the conversation was cut short by a blast of profanity from the men's quarters.

"What in the . . ." Luc bounded out the door.

Katherine and Clive followed, arriving just in time to see Shorty Johnson tumble unceremoniously onto the snow-packed roadside. Redbeard Simpson thundered after the little man, grabbing him by the shirt, jerking him upright, and shaking him like a dishrag in the wind. "Don't you ever mess around my bunk again."

With a flip of the wrist, Redbeard flung Shorty into the snow-bank a second time.

Shorty picked himself up, snorting and swinging his fists in unyielding frustration. "It's mine and you know it." A torrent of profanity issued from the depths of Shorty's gut.

By now the entire camp had assembled.

Luc Dubois strode forward, towering over the scene, legs aspread and hands on hips. The muscles in his jaw rippled and his barrel chest swelled under his green plaid shirt. He glared down from his six-foot-ten inches, red-faced and smoldering.

"What's going on here?" he roared. Reaching out, he held his hand palm up. "Redbeard, what-a-you got?"

Everyone waited, staring in dead silence at the scene before them.

Redbeard glared back with fists convulsing.

Luc stood mute, muscles flexed and ready. "Do you need me to prove who's boss?"

Anxiety and dread filled the air.

Redbeard's jaw flexed, and his knuckles turned white. Finally he reached into his McMillans and pulled out a silver pocket watch, its chain dangling over his palm. He dropped it into Luc's hand and backed slowly toward the bunkhouse.

Luc handed the watch to Shorty and walked away.

Katherine and the others stood awestruck at the towering presence of the man.

The next day, Readbeard Simpson picked up his time check and left camp.

CHAPTER FIFTEEN

It was Monday morning, and Frank rode with Jasper on the swing dingle. They were to deliver lunch to the lumberjacks in the woods. Angus had pumped hot water into the reservoir that surrounded the food compartment, Hannah and Angus had loaded the shelves with food, and Henri LeBlanc had hitched the horse to the sleigh. Jasper held the reins as they slid over the snowy ground.

Arriving at the site, Frank found that the fire they'd built earlier had burned down to a bed of coals, warm but with no smoke to blow in the men's faces. The jacks stood near the fire, turning front to back, warming first one side and then the other.

Not far away the logging horses stood under a sheltering tree, where Klaus had stationed them. They were covered with blankets and eating oats from their nosebags. They must be fed and kept warm so they would be refreshed for the afternoon's work.

As the sleigh came to a stop, Jasper hopped onto the ground. He opened the food box, exposing a wall of shelves with hot food kept that way by the reservoir of nearly boiling water surrounding it. Inside was a veritable feast for the jacks—roast beef and mashed potatoes, baked beans and carrots and rutabagas—with rolls and cake and pudding.

The crew fell into line filling their plates and seating themselves on a log. All was silent as they gulped their food, and by twelve thirty they were headed back to the worksite.

Frank and Jasper closed the swing dingle and climbed aboard for the return trip to camp.

The day was cold but sunny, and they moved rapidly over the snow, arriving in due time at the Jordan River where great mounds of new-fallen snow lay like fluffy clouds of cotton atop a host of dead branches that had fallen into the water over the years. The river rushed forward, tumbling over itself as if trying to escape the icy environs that should have frozen it solid.

Near Wetwater Rapids, Jasper flicked the reins and turned the rig north, traveling away from the bank and into the deep woods.

"Jasper," Frank said, "how long have you been doing this kind of thing? Do you ever think about getting a job that's not so dangerous?"

"Oh yes, don't we all?" Jasper shrugged. "But this is what I was born to. Pa did it before me, and I just kind of fell into it."

"Well, I've been thinking about Tom Morse over in Camp Paulson. One day he's alive and healthy and the next day a bunkload of logs gets out of hand, skids down the ice road, and runs over him. What happens to his widow? Do you suppose she'll take the kids and go back to Scotland?"

"Probably not. They usually just live out their lives in the States. She may marry again or she may not."

Frank fell silent, pondering a world where son follows father into a life where death lurks ever at the door.

Suddenly Jasper jerked the reins. "Look out," he yelled. "There's a . . ."

A loud crack reverberated through the air, and Jasper's voice exploded into the void. "Whoa!"

The next thing Frank knew, he was lying in the wanigan. His entire body throbbed, his head ached, and his breath came in wispy pants. Luc and Jasper stood over him, and he could hear their voices in the distance. "Widow-maker swung down out of the tree and walloped him aside the head. Smacked him right out of the rig and into them cussed rocks. He didn't have a chance."

"I don't think he's going to make it."

It was Luc, leaning over him with his hand resting on Frank's shoulder.

Frank heard no more.

Two days later, Katherine sat by Uncle Ned's table with Uncle Ned, Aunt Mae, and Parson Tibbs. Frank lay in a pine box at the church, his body smashed and broken. Aunt Mae reached out and touched Katherine's arm.

"Don't worry, Katherine. You'll be OK. Your Uncle Ned and I are here for you and the girls."

All at once, the anger and resentment of a lifetime flared. "I don't want to be mollycoddled," she spat. "I want my husband." Aunt Mae dropped her hand. Time froze in steely silence, until at last Parson Tibbs spoke. "Just leave the burden with God, Katherine. He knows and He cares."

"Who says God cares?" Katherine slapped the table with her fist. "He's taken every good thing I ever had in life and you tell me He cares? He doesn't care. He hates me. And I hate Him."

"No, Katherine, you don't hate God." Pain echoed in Parson Tibbs' voice. "God is your source of strength. We don't know why these things happen, but we do know that God cares, and He'll help you through these trying times."

Katherine collapsed onto the table and let the tears flow. Parson Tibbs and the others sat nearby, allowing the pain to spill forth.

Aunt Mae handed Katherine a handkerchief, which she wadded into a ball and squeezed with all her might.

In time, the parson stood. He laid his hand on Katherine's shoulder. "I have to go now but I'll be close by if you need me."

Katherine raised her head and wiped her eyes with Aunt Mae's hanky.

Uncle Ned saw the pastor to the door.

After many long minutes, Katherine rose and wandered dully into the parlor. There she dropped onto the divan and cried herself into a stupor. All day long the tears surged just under the surface, and she slept deeply that night.

The next day Katherine combed her hair into a bun, put on Aunt Mae's black hat, and pulled her coat over her shoulders. She gathered the fabric pieces that would have become Frank's homecoming quilt and tucked them inside, close to her heart.

Then she kissed Faith Ann goodbye. "Auntie Emma has come to play with you," she said, "so be a good girl, and I'll be back after while." A lost emptiness filled Katherine's chest, as she stepped outdoors into an icy gale. She climbed onto Uncle Ned's sleigh with Hannah and Aunt Mae. Uncle Ned flicked the reins and the horses trotted down the lane toward the church.

Arriving at their destination, Katherine composed herself, walking with Hannah and Aunt Mae down the aisle to the second pew where Jasper already sat. Time passed in silence; the presence of death permeated the atmosphere.

Finally, the clock struck three and Irene Radley began to sing. "Nearer, my God, to Thee, Nearer to Thee!"

Katherine sat unresponsive in a cold, empty abyss. "E'en though it be a cross that raiseth me."

As the last notes faded away, Pastor Tibbs moved to the platform.

"Today we come to honor Frank McLean," he said. "Since the day I met Frank, it was obvious to me that his greatest desire was to be a good provider for his family."

The parson spoke of Frank's shoe shop that came to a tragic end. He spoke of Frank's goal to spend this one winter in the woods and then set up a business in Hitchcock.

"May God receive his soul and comfort those whom he left behind," he said at last.

The congregation was dismissed, but Katherine stayed behind, waiting to be alone with her companion. She stood in the empty church, peering through her tears at the figure in the pine box—her husband, her source of strength, an empty image of the man she loved. With aching heart she pulled the hearts and rings from her breast.

"I'll miss you, Frank," she whispered. "But I'll take good care of your girls. I'll find a way."

She tucked the quilt pieces into the box beside Frank's body. "Goodbye, my love," she whispered. "Goodbye."

She closed the lid and turned to go.

Later that day Frank's body would be deposited in the village icehouse to remain until the ground thawed in the spring.

Clive hunkered down in his mackinaw, pulling his arms close to his sides for warmth. He bent his head and leaned into the storm, hurrying along the tote road toward Camp DuBois.

"Burrrrr," he hollered as he burst into the cook shanty. "It's cold enough out there to freeze the hair off a brass mule."

Angus Muldoon stood in the kitchen, spewing epithets at everything that walked and most things that didn't. "They say the soup tastes like last week's wash water. Well, if they don't like it, let 'em come in here and cook fer their selves."

"Top o' the mornin' to you, Angus," Clive called.

Angus wiped his hands on his apron. "Cussed camp's gone mad. And if that woman doesn't come back soon and take over this job, I'm gonna walk right out of here and never be seen again. Jake is about as much help as a bee on the back of a mule. He won't do dishes, and he hollers every time he has to serve a meal."

Jake Emmonds, the old jack who served the camp as handyman, appeared in the doorway. "Well, oh yeah? If you don't like, it you c'n just do the job yerself. I didn't come here to be nobody's houseboy. I agreed to help 'til Emma gets back, but I didn't agree to be yer whippin' boy."

Angus slapped a cover onto a twenty-gallon pot and walked into the dining area carrying a plate full of stale sourdough bread.

"If ya want sweet rolls, ye'll have to wait 'til Emma gets back," he sputtered. "I don't make no special stuff fer these snivelin' gully-whumpers."

Jake poured three cups of coffee and took a seat at the table with Clive and Angus.

They'd no more than lifted their cups, when Luc came through the door. He threw his mackinaw in a corner and plopped onto the bench. "This is just what we need, a lousy blizzard to drop its fury all over the place."

He poured a cup of coffee. "We got three million feet of logs out there to fell and the whole camp's gotta go tramp skidways. It'll be days before we can go back to work. There'll be logs buried so deep in this stuff we'll never get 'em out." Luc bristled as he gulped the coffee.

Clive turned on his seat. "So what's going on, Luc . . . outside of this blow, of course. Where's Emma?"

"Lousy widow-maker swung down from a tree and knocked Frank McLean off the swing dingle." Luc's jaws ground together, rigid and unyielding. "He was killed."

"What? Frank McLean was . . ."

Before Clive could finish, a loud whinny echoed through the camp, accompanied by a frenzy of curses that would scare a bull.

"Now what?"

Luc bolted out the door with Clive close behind. "What's goin' on out here?"

There in the road stood Klause Bruner hitching his team to the vee-plow. "Bitchin' nag jibed and got me in the back."

Klause went about his work, grumbling constantly and calling down vengeance from heaven on "that cussed nag." Then, when the vee-plow was ready, Klause leaped aboard and snapped the reins. The vee-plow, made of split logs stacked several feet high on its frame, would be hauled over the tote road day and night until the storm was over. And the roads would be clear.

Clive and Luc went back inside, gulped their coffee, and headed out on the jumper to check the camp. Snow whirled past in a race with time.

"So, Luc, tell me about Frank. What happened?"

Luc went over the events of Frank's death. "Poor Katherine was devastated. I thought she was going to lose it when his frozen body was loaded onto the tote wagon. There was just nothing I could do to make it easier."

"And Hannah and Faith Ann—how are they taking it?"

"Hannah's probably at least as upset as Katherine, having lost her ma some years back, but Faith Ann just seems lost. She keeps asking, where is her pa."

Clive's heart went out to Katherine and her girls. How could this have happened? If anyone deserved something good in life, it surely was she.

Making their way through the blinding snow, Clive and Luc arrived at the first logging site, where they found a dozen or so lumberjacks tramping up and down through the swirling snow. In times like this, the skidways must be tramped constantly to maintain an even surface through the woods. If there was anything the camp did not need it was a horse made lame due to a stumble on a rough logging trail. Horses were the life of the camp, and they must be protected.

Clive and Luc spent considerable time encouraging the jacks and overseeing the operation. Then Luc flicked the reins, and the horses moved out toward the next location.

For the next three days and nights, the wind blew and the snow fell. And for the next three days and nights, the jacks cleared the roads in shifts. Then, on the morning of the fourth day, the snow let up, the sun came out and Camp DuBois went back to work. Sawyers would hew the great pines and swampers would clear away branches and prepare logs for skidding. Logs would be hauled to the riverbank and decked to await the spring thaw.

The storm that had blasted the area after Frank's death let up and Katherine returned to Camp DuBois to finish Frank's year as clerk. Just now she sat in the wanigan, peering between the icicles that stood from ground to eaves outside her window. The land lay knee-deep in a blanket of newfallen snow, and the ever present pines reached a hundred feet into the sky.

Today the sprinkler crew was out rebuilding the damaged ice roads, and when the new layer of ice was frozen solid, the rut cutters would retrench. By tomorrow the road would be repaired and the logging sleighs would glide smoothly along the ruts with their heavy loads.

The bunkhouse, where the jacks slept on narrow bunks covered with straw and infested with bugs, stood across the road just north of the wanigan. The barn, the blacksmith shop, and the filer's shanty lay to the south. The cook shanty stood directly across the way.

Surrounding the camp on all sides were the giant pines that had enticed the jacks to enter this virgin country in the first place. The trees stood tall and regal, reaching 150 feet in the air on trunks that were three or more feet across, whispering their secrets to the wind. It was said that you could build a house with just one of those great trees.

Katherine made her way across the road to the cook shanty. She needed Emma's order for the tote teamster.

"Emma, do you have my order ready?" she called.

"It's right here on the counter, waiting for you to come by." Suddenly, Jake Emmonds burst through the door and threw his hat at the table, allowing his bowl-cut gray hair to stick out in every direction. He stood muttering about the lamebrain who was always running off with his tools. Everyone knew the problem was Jake's own forgetfulness, but no one said a word.

Luc and Jasper sat at the table drinking coffee, and the smile that spread across Luc's face told the story of Jake's problem.

"When I was a hewer, a man's tools were his own," Jake carped. "Ya didn't have every Tom, Dick, and Harry a-grabbin' yer stuff and leavin' it layin' all over the place."

Luc nodded in peremptory finality. "Come on, Jake, sit down and have coffee with me and Jasper. Those tools'll turn up in a day or two. In the meantime you can repair harnesses."

Jake threw up his hands. "How do you expect a man to get anything done around here if the jacks won't leave his stuff alone?"

Luc smiled. "Well, Jake, don't worry about it. Just sit down here and say hello to Katherine."

Jake stopped short, lifted one leg and then the other over the bench and seated himself beside Luc at the long lumber camp table. "G'mornin'."

His face remained frozen in a grimace, and Katherine knew he'd been instructed to hold his tongue when she was around. In fact, all of the jacks treated her with respect and even warm regard.

Katherine had found Luc to be more considerate than she'd ever thought possible. Although he had the power to whip anyone in camp, and he ruled with a powerful fist, he seemed somehow out of place in this raucous world. His black hair and beard were neatly trimmed and his flannel shirts and McMillan trousers always looked clean—no small feat for a man of the deep woods.

After several minutes, Katherine took her leave. "I'd like to stay and visit," she said, "but I have to get this order ready." She excused herself and made her way across the road to the wanigan.

"Mama," Faith Ann yelled, as Katherine entered, "Hannah won't let me see her pin. She's got it out and she won't even let me touch it."

The little girl yanked at her mother's skirt. "She says it's from Grandma McLean and it's hers and I can't even look at it." Katherine sighed. "Hannah, would it hurt you to let Faith Ann touch that pin?"

Hannah whipped her head around, glaring at her little sister. "I don't want her thinking she can play with my brooch any old time she wants to. She did it before, and she better not do it again."

"Hannah, let her touch the brooch, for Pete's sake. And then, Faith Ann, you leave it alone."

Katherine stepped behind the counter, pulling the gate shut behind her. This was all she needed on a day when she was up to her ears in bookkeeping.

Hannah held out the brooch. "Oh all right." She held the pin, as Faith Ann brushed her hand over the golden whorls. "But don't you ever touch it, when I'm not holding it."

Hannah slipped the ornament into its black velvet bag, pulled the drawstring tight, and deposited it in her case.

Just then the door opened and Clive entered. "Hannah, do you have your arithmetic book out so we can get started with your ciphering?"

Hannah's face lit up like she'd just gone to heaven. "Yes, Clive, the books are right here."

She opened her book and flipped through the pages. Clive pulled up a chair, and the two sat side by side at the desk.

"Look here," Hannah said. "I don't understand why . . . ."

The voices grew soft, and Katherine couldn't make out their meaning. For nearly a half hour Clive and Hannah sat side by side, almost touching. Hannah obviously enjoyed the experience a great deal.

Katherine supposed the girl might need help with her ciphering, and she had agreed to the arrangement, but she wasn't sure she liked this relationship one bit.

In time, Clive rose to his feet. "OK, you got that. Now just do those problems in the back of the book, and I'll try to get back before too long to work on the next lesson."

Clive talked aimlessly to Katherine for several long minutes, shifting from one foot to the other, as if there were something on his mind that he wasn't discussing.

Well, Katherine thought, *he'd better not ask for more time with Hannah, because I'm not about to permit it.*

Chapter Sixteen

Katherine sat in the wanigan, resting after a long day of checking stock and recording totals. The girls had retired for the night, and she sat in quiet solitude reliving her promise to Frank.

She leaned back, closed her eyes, and sighed.

She'd just put the books away, when she heard a light rap on the door. "Come in," she called.

"Katherine, do you have time for a visit?" It was Clive.

He took a seat and looked deeply into her eyes. "How are you doing? I mean . . ."

Katherine swallowed the lump in her throat. "I guess we'll make it. We have to stay in camp this one winter. Then, come spring, we'll build a house on Uncle Ned's farm. I'll bake bread and rolls to sell at Hitchcock's, and we'll do all right."

"Well, I've been thinking about you and your girls, and I have an idea. What if I told you there's a woman with a teenage daughter who lives nearby. They're alone most of the time, because the husband and father is off tending his trap lines. I know Maggie would enjoy getting to know you, and Hannah just might like to have a friend her own age."

Katherine pursed her lips, to control her quivering chin.

"Name's Nilsson. They're fine people, and I think you'd like them."

"Yes, let's do it soon."

The next Sunday, Katherine and her girls walked with Clive along the tote road toward Maggie Nilsson's home. Bright sunshine reflected off the snow, producing one of those uncommonly warm February days. Birds twittered in the trees and coats hung open as the four friends walked along. Faith Ann hung on her mother's arm, chattering constantly, while Clive and Hannah walked several steps ahead, deep in some discussion. Clive leaned down gesturing with his fingers. Hannah looked up at Clive, smiling and nodding.

Katherine grimaced. Surely Clive wouldn't let himself become involved with a young teenage girl. He was a grown man, almost twice Hannah's age. Yet Clive was very good looking. He had an infectious personality, and Hannah was obviously taken with him.

Katherine breathed deeply of the spring-like air and pushed the thought to the back of her mind, preferring to think Clive just wanted to be friends with her family.

"Clive," she called out, "how long have these folks been living out here?"

Clive slowed his pace, falling into step with Katherine.

"I'm not sure—for quite a long while, though. Max has a pretty clear claim on his trap line."

Clive walked along beside her, and he seemed perfectly content to have left off his discussion with Hannah. Katherine assured herself that she'd been too critical; Clive wouldn't mess with her daughter.

In time, Katherine and her family arrived at the cuttings, that great backdrop of stumps and brush that had been left by the lumbermen. A tarpaper house stood along the tree line some distance off the road, with a pathway leading to it through the snow.

"That's the Nilssons'," Clive said, pointing. "Hannah, you go first. Katherine and Faith Ann can come after, and I'll bring up the rear."

Hannah stepped into the narrow opening between the drifts, and the others followed marching single file toward the little cabin.

As they drew near, a big, yellow dog bounded out the door followed by a girl about Hannah's age, though taller, somewhat thinner, and deeply tanned. The girl's brown hair was tied in a knot and held in place with a scrap of yellow cloth.

"Sabaka, come here," the girl called.

The dog stopped, looking back as though not sure of its next move.

"Sabaka, I said come."

The dog retreated a few steps and waited. The girl broke into a run. "Mr. Clive."

"Willowbelle."

Clive stepped forward as the pathway widened. "I brought a friend for you. This is Hannah McLean. She's spending the winter at the DuBois camp."

Willowbelle's face broke into a smile. "Hannah, it's really good to meet you. I always wished I had someone my own age to talk to."

Just then, an older woman with salt-and-pepper gray hair and tanned skin stepped outside. "Willow, get back here. I told you . . ."

The woman stopped. Brushing her hand over her apron, she moved toward Clive and his friends. "Well, Clive Isaman, it's good to see you again. And who is this you've got with you?"

"Maggie, this is Katherine McLean, and these are her daughters, Hannah and Faith Ann. They're over at the DuBois camp for the winter, and I thought you might like to meet them."

"Well, let's go inside; shall we?"

Maggie led the way into a modest living area, picking up a pair of overalls that lay over a chair and hanging them on a nail by the door. "Can I offer you coffee?"

"Sure," Clive volunteered.

Maggie cleared breakfast dishes from the table and set out mugs for three adults.

Willowbelle reached for her coat. "I think I'll take Hannah out to see the place, OK?"

"OK, but don't go too far. Stay within hearing distance, you hear?"

"We will."

The girls disappeared out the door.

Maggie was easy to talk to, and Katherine soon found herself in deep discussion of women's needs and desires and the importance of family and the need of security for their children.

Clive sat on the settee with Faith Ann, drumming his fingers on the armrest. "Come on, Faith Ann," he said. "They don't seem to need us."

He rose, took Faith Ann by the hand, and moved toward the door.

Katherine's heart fluttered. Her baby looked perfectly happy walking hand in hand with her father. Sometimes life took strange turns.

"I'm right in the middle of a batch of bread," Maggie said. "C'mon out in the kitchen while I shape the loaves."

She drained the last of her coffee and led the way out of the living area into a simple kitchen with crudely built counters and cabinets. The walls were decorated with magazine pictures. There were pictures of grand homes with manicured lawns, images of sparkling lakes with fine yachts, and there were pictures of beautiful ladies wearing exquisite dresses, obviously cut from the Sears catalog. A cookstove stood along the south wall, emanating warmth throughout the room.

"I'm really glad you came," Maggie said. She patted and rolled a wad of dough until it became a loaf. "I worry that Willowbelle is alone out here too much. It'll be good for her to have a friend." She laid the loaf in a pan to rise.

"We'll have to see to it that the girls get together often," Katherine responded.

As the women talked, Katherine spoke of Frank's death in a way she hadn't before. Maggie knew what it was to be alone in the world with a child to care for, and Katherine felt a bond with the woman.

Maggie told of her loneliness with Max gone most of the time. She talked of his nights in the forest and the shelters he'd found where he spent his nights.

"But he got the surprise of his life the last time he was out," Maggie said. "There's this old stone house near Hitchcock, where he likes to sleep when he's in the area."

Katherine's heart skipped a beat.

"But the last time he stopped, the place was locked up tighter'n a drum. He had to sleep in the barn."

Katherine gulped. "The Beasley place?" "Yes. How did you know?"

"Maggie, I was in the house that night. He nearly scared me to death."

Maggie's eyebrows shot upward.

"Max came home that next week madder'n a hatter. Said if he ever found the bloke who locked that door he'd tar 'n' feather 'em."

Katherine gulped. "I hope he didn't mean it."

"Nah." Maggie grinned. "He's over it by now. And even if he weren't, he'll never find out."

Clive walked around the Nilsson place hand in hand with Faith Ann. What a sweet little girl Katherine had brought into the world. And now she had no pa. He almost wished he could make her his own.

But that would never do. He spent entirely too much time in the woods to ever be anyone's pa. He'd play with the little girl today, and she'd be his for the moment; then he'd be on his way. Bending down, he grabbed a fistful of snow. "Let's make a snow fort."

Faith Ann grabbed a wad of snow. "I like to make a snow fort."

Together Clive and Faith Ann stacked snowballs in a row to make a wall. Soon Willow and Hannah noticed the activity and came running to join the fun. They rolled snowballs in the melting snow, leaving wide paths of bare earth. They placed the snowballs together, stacking them atop one another and smoothing the sides. They formed turrets on the corners and used an old board over the door. They even made a stockpile of cannon balls out of snow to throw at make-believe enemies.

And then it happened. Clive turned and a snowball smashed into his chest.

"Gotcha," Hannah called.

"Now you did it."

Clive grabbed a handful of snow and tossed it back at the girl. Soon everyone was enmeshed in a rousing snowball fight. They threw snow and laughed and played. And too soon it was time to leave.

"I don't know when I've had such a nice day," Maggie said. "Thank you, Clive, for bringing Katherine and the girls. And, Katherine, I hope we'll see you again soon."

"You will, Maggie. You will."

Walking back along the tote road toward camp, Clive moved near to Hannah, resuming their conversation of the morning. What a stroke of luck. Hannah had asked him to help her study arithmetic. He had agreed, knowing it would give him a perfect excuse to be near Katherine and her family. Maybe he could build a relationship with Katherine and help her overcome the pain of losing her husband.

Chapter Seventeen

Hannah sat at her study table, working on her arithmetic and thinking of Clive. It was just yesterday he'd been in camp and already she missed him. She really liked Clive; he was so good looking—and smart about ciphering too. He'd said he'd stop by often to see how she was doing, and she could hardly wait for his return.

And there was Willowbelle. What luck! Hannah hadn't imagined there would be a friend for her in the woods. But there she was, just across the way. Willow, that was her nickname, was real smart. She liked to read, and she had books all over the place, maybe half a dozen or so. Someone got her started, but basically she just learned all by herself. Hannah was going back to the cabin soon to teach Willow about ciphering.

As Hannah sat reveling in her good fortune, the door opened and Luc entered, ducking his head as usual to avoid slamming it on the doorjamb.

"Mornin', Hannah. Where's Katherine? There's someone I'd like her to meet."

Hannah looked up and just about fell off her chair. There in full habit stood a nun. What in the world was a nun doing out here?

Katherine appeared from behind the counter where she'd been working, and Hannah could see by the look on her face that Katherine was as startled as she herself had been.

"Yes?"

"Katherine, I'd like you to meet Sister Olivia." Luc turned to the nun. "Sister, this is the woman I told you about. She's been a real help to the camp."

"Good morning, Mrs. McLean." The nun reached out her hand. "It's quite a surprise to find a woman in camp."

"You're a bit of a surprise yourself." Katherine extended her hand to the nun.

"I come to the camps every year to provide the jacks with hospital tickets. A lot of them buy the tickets; that way if they're injured, they can go to the hospital for the care they need."

Sister Olivia nodded in Hannah's direction. "And who might this young woman be?"

"This is my daughter, Hannah."

A swell of pleasure trickled up Hannah's spine. Only a short time ago she'd have resented Katherine claiming to be her mother, but since that big fight they'd had while gathering eggs, things had begun to get better. And since Pa died, it seemed like Hannah and Katherine had developed a real friendship. Katherine had lost her mother, too, and she understood about the emptiness that never goes away.

"It's nice to meet you, Sister," Hannah said.

Faith Ann pulled back the curtain and came out of the sleeping area, looking up at the sister with bewilderment.

"Sister, this is my youngest daughter," Katherine said. "Say hello to Sister Olivia, Faith Ann."

Sister Olivia reached out with a flourish. "Well, hello there, little girl. I haven't seen such a pretty face since I came into these woods."

Faith Ann puffed herself up to full height. "I'm a big girl. I'm almost five."

"Yes, you are a big girl," the sister agreed. "I can see that now."

Luc stepped forward, looking down from his nearly seven-foot height. "Katherine, Sister Olivia will need a place to sleep tonight. I expect she'll sleep here with you."

"Certainly," Katherine responded.

Hannah almost fell over. There'd be no privacy at all behind that curtain.

Luc looked pleased. "Good. Then that's taken care of. Now, Sister, shall we go back to the cook shanty for coffee? And Katherine, why don't you come along and get acquainted."

"OK, Luc, I'll be there in a minute, soon's I get this box unpacked."

"So now what?" Hannah said, after Luc and the sister had gone. "Where'll we put her?"

"We'll work out something," Katherine responded. "Maybe you could sleep on the bottom bunk with the sister, and Faith Ann and I will sleep on the top bunk."

Katherine finished what she was doing and rounded the counter, heading for the door. "At any rate, I'm going over for coffee now. Keep an eye on Faith Ann, will you?"

After Katherine left, Hannah returned to her studies, but her mind just wouldn't stay on track. All she could think about was the realization that she must sleep with the sister tonight. She'd never seen a sister without her habit before, let alone in her nightgown. Hannah must spend the night with a nun—who would not be dressed, and who would be in Hannah's bed—with Hannah.

Then inspiration struck. What about Willow? Maybe Hannah could go to the Nilssons' cabin for the night. She and Willow would probably have to sleep together, but that was a lot better than sleeping with an undressed nun. She'd take her books and paper and Willow could start learning to cipher. It was perfect all the way around.

Later, Hannah told Katherine about her idea and it was agreed that it would work. Indeed, Katherine seemed pleased. "Only one thing," she said. "Old Jake must escort you through the woods."

Hannah heaved a sigh of relief and grabbed a pillowcase. She stuffed her nightgown into it, along with a comb and a pencil and paper and her arithmetic book. The bag looked a little like the turkeys the jacks brought with them when they arrived at camp in the fall.

"C'n I go too, Mama?" Faith Ann looked up at Katherine with pleading eyes. "C'n I go?"

"I don't know, sweetheart," Katherine said. "You're kind of little to go to a stranger's house overnight, especially without an invitation."

"I'm not a little girl. I'm big."

"And what would you do at the Nilssons'? There's no one for you to play with over there."

Hannah broke in. "Actually, I think it might be a good idea. Mrs. Nilsson really likes company. She'd likely spend the whole time playing with Faith Ann instead of working, and you and the sister could have more privacy that way. And if she can't stay, she can come back with Jake."

Katherine shrugged. "Well, OK, she can go, but keep an eye on her. And if she gets to be a problem, she's your responsibility."

Faith Ann clapped her hands and pirouetted around the room singing, "I get to go. I get to go. I get to go with Hannah." Then she stopped in her tracks. "I gotta get a turkey," she said. And she ran behind the curtain.

At the Nilssons' cabin, things were as Hannah had predicted. At first sight, Willow came running to meet them. Then Maggie nearly hugged the life out of poor Faith Ann, and she treated Jake like a long-lost brother. She laid out coffee and fresh bread with honey, insisting he visit for a while.

Jake agreed, feigning reluctance, and took a seat. He availed himself of a slice of bread, buttered it well, and spread it generously with honey. He and Maggie talked of old times in the woods and how things had changed.

Finally, late in the afternoon, Jake took his leave. "I'll be back for you girls in the morning, so don't leave without me," he admonished.

"Goodbye Jake," Maggie called, as the old handyman strode down the lane. "It was good visiting with you."

Then she smiled and turned her attention to Faith Ann. "C'mon," she said. "Let's go see if Lulu will let you go for a ride." Faith Ann charged out the door with Maggie in close pursuit. "OK," Hannah said to Willow after they'd gone. "You want to try your hand at ciphering?"

Willow grinned. "Let's. I'm really eager to get started."

So Hannah copied a few basic problems from her book, solved one of them as an example, and gave the paper to Willow.

"OK, it's your turn. If you have a question, just ask me." Then before Hannah really got started with her own ciphering, Willow had solved all of the equations. The next set of problems was more difficult.

Hannah sat for some time poring over her work, when a soft groan across the table caught her attention. "Willow, are you OK?"

Hannah peered at Willow. The girl's face was ashen. She looked as if she were about to faint.

"Willow, what is it?"

Willow held her breath for several seconds and then let it out in a long, measured sigh. Tears seeped from her eyes.

"Willow, what's the matter?" Hannah leaned over her friend, brushing the young woman's shoulders.

"I don't know," Willow said at last. "I've been getting these terrible headaches, and they just seem to get worse and worse. I'm afraid Ma's going to find out one of these times, and it'll worry her to death."

"Your ma doesn't know? Willow, you can't keep a thing like that from your ma."

"If Ma ever finds out, it'll drive her crazy. She can't know. Promise me you won't tell. There's nothing to be done about it, and there's no point in worrying her."

"Willow, I can't promise a thing like that."

"You gotta; Ma'd worry herself right into the grave."

"And you? Are you going to your grave without telling her?" "OK, I'll tell her, but you let me do it."

"All right, but get it done. She needs to know."

Hannah laid her studies aside and sat with Willow on the settee, wishing there were some way she could ease her friend's pain.

Back at the camp, Katherine sat with Luc on a bench in the men's quarters. Jacks perched on benches and bunks all along the south end of the room.

Near the center stood an old potbellied stove with several wires strung above it. The smelly socks that usually hung over the wires had been relegated to the back of the building. In the morning the washerman, a rarity in the camps, would pick them up for cleaning.

Sister Olivia stood near the stove, commanding everyone's attention. A deep, throaty tune wafted through the room with no accompaniment:

"Amazing grace, how sweet the sound that saved a wretch like me. I once was lost but now I'm found, was blind but now I see." As the song drew to a close, Sister Olivia's face tipped downward in reverence and the last note drifted into nothingness. A single pair of hands clapped. And then another, and another, until the room was filled with applause.

"Hey Jake," someone hollered, "why don't you play your fiddle for the sister?"

Jake rose and made his way out the door. His fiddle was, most likely, in the cook shanty.

The sister raised her hand for silence. "How many of you know Dan Parker from Camp Mishkin?"

Shoulders shifted and several hands were raised.

"You'll remember he was badly wounded last fall by a widowmaker that swung down and grazed his back. Well, he's getting better, but he's still in the hospital. And thanks to his hospital ticket, he'll be able to stay until his back is healed."

The sister shifted positions and went on. "And today I've come to supply or renew your hospital tickets. They'll be good this winter and next, until I come again. It's a dollar and a half, and you'll be protected, as Dan was."

The sister looked around the room, making eye contact with the jacks. "Do you ever wonder why I tramp across the snow, using whatever means I can to bring these tickets to you?"

She stood silent for several seconds, allowing the query to sink in. "Well, mine is a mission of love. God has given me this assignment because he cares for you. For God is love."

God is love, Katherine thought. *Well, I haven't seen much of that.*

"The fact is that your lives are pretty rugged out here. Men get hurt. They get sick with the cold. Families are left behind. But God didn't say you'd have it easy."

Katherine's brow furrowed. How did the sister know what she was thinking?

"What He has promised is that He'll be there to help you." The sister went on to say that problems can make your spirit grow strong, just like working your muscles makes them grow strong.

"So problems will come, but when they do, God sends His Spirit to help. Sometimes He works through another person; sometimes He speaks to you directly. Or He may work in other ways."

A short pause—total silence.

"And you grow strong in the process."

Sister Olivia prayed. Then she took a seat on the bench, and the jacks formed a line to renew their tickets. A few paid with cash, but most chose to have Katherine deduct the cost from their pay.

Finally the sales were finished, and the sister stood. Old Jake, now armed with his fiddle, stepped to her side. His bow glided across the strings, and strains of "Blessed Assurance" filled the room. The sister sang, and when the song was finished she took a seat on the bench.

Jake then swung into a round of "Turkey in the Straw," Gus Erickson whipped out his harmonica, and the jacks' feet began tapping to the music. Soon the men were singing and clapping in rhythm. Sister Olivia sat on the bench with Katherine, mending the jacks' socks.

Later Katherine and the sister made their way to the wanigan, where Sister Olivia removed her head cover. The sister's cheeks, which looked so plump and round in the habit, softened, and a comeliness emerged that Katherine hadn't noticed before. Dark hair framed her face in a mass of curls. She glowed with a beauty that expressed itself in pure, free-spirited joy.

Sister Olivia laid her covering over a chair and breathed a deep sigh. "It certainly is nice to spend the night with another woman," she said. "You'd be surprised at some of the sleeping arrangements I've seen."

Katherine smiled. Sister Olivia was cut from a special bolt of cloth, and Katherine would not soon forget this night. She slipped behind the counter, wrote a voucher to cover cost of the jacks' hospital tickets, and gave it to Sister Olivia. Then the two women sat together near the stove, discussing good times and bad. Katherine told the story of her life and how her dreams were always swept away just as they came within her grasp.

"How can you say God loves me, when He treats me this way?" she asked.

"Only you can answer that," the sister responded. "Sometimes God allows pain to enter our lives to help us grow into people of better character. Or perhaps you are yet to learn the skill or lesson He has for you. Perhaps you are destined to be a special blessing for someone at sometime. Have you examined your situation with intent to find His plan for your life?"

Katherine sat in quiet meditation for some time. "No, I guess I haven't."

She rose and pulled back the privacy curtain, still ruminating over the sister's query. "It's getting late; perhaps we should turn in."

"That's a good idea. It's been a long day and I'll be visiting Camp Mishkin tomorrow."

"You can sleep on the bottom bunk," Katherine said. "I'll sleep on the top."

"Nothing doing," the sister replied. "I'll take the top."

Katherine donned her nightgown, careful not to see the sister, who was removing her habit in favor of nightclothes.

Then Sister Olivia grabbed the top rung of the ladder, lifted a foot onto the second step, and flew onto the bunk in a single leap.

Katherine stood in awe.

When both were ready, Katherine blew into the lamp's chimney to extinguish the flame and climbed into bed. She lay for many minutes, considering Sister Olivia's insight. What was

Katherine's mission in life? She'd really never considered that she might have one.

Some time later, night shadows descended.

In the morning Katherine rose, pulled on her clothes, and checked the fire. A bed of coals still smoldered in the pot, and she tossed several sticks of kindling on top. When the kindling burst into flame, she tossed in larger pieces, and soon a warm fire poured heat into the room. She stood near the heater, warming her hands, when the sister emerged from behind the curtain, fully dressed in her habit. Together they made their way across the road to the cook shanty.

"Good day, ladies," Luc said as they entered. "Did you have a good night?"

The sister assured him she had slept well and nodded good morning to Jake and the tote teamster who sat at breakfast.

Katherine and the sister took their places at the table, and Angus brought coffee and hot cakes with bacon. Katherine helped herself to one of Emma's good pancakes, and was about to pour maple syrup when she noticed the sister crossing herself. She waited and then doused her meal with the treacle.

I like this lady, Katherine thought. *She's genuine. She lives what she believes.*

An hour and a half later, Sister Olivia climbed onto the wagon with the tote teamster.

"It was nice visiting with you," she called.

The teamster flicked the reins and the horses stepped out. Katherine waved until the wagon rounded the bend and disappeared. She thought about what the sister said. Was God really trying to teach her something? If so, what? Did she really have a mission in life? It was an interesting new concept for Katherine.

CHAPTER EIGHTEEN

The entire population of Camp DuBois was abuzz. Tomorrow the jacks would construct their entry for the countywide loading contest. If the load won, it would be entered in a statewide competition whose winner would be transported by rail to the State Fair in Detroit.

Photojournalist Thomas Lind would arrive on the tote wagon today to photograph the event and write a report for the Charlevoix Times. Yuri Tomich, the county scaler, would also be in camp to record the number of board-feet in the load. Clive was coming in on foot, and there would be locals visiting from nearby cabins. Even Don Parker, cruiser for Waterhouse Lumber, had dropped by, having finished his survey of the Upper Peninsula.

Katherine heaped a pile of writing pads on the shelf behind the counter. The shelves must be full on loading day, because the jacks would be in to pick up personal items while they had the day off work. Of course that meant Katherine must spend most of the day in the wanigan, but she would be free to watch the loading itself.

Hannah and Faith Ann had been at the Nilssons' cabin since Friday, and Katherine supposed Maggie was spending every minute with Faith Ann playing house or gathering eggs or whatever—and spoiling the child rotten in the process. The girls would be arriving early with Maggie and Willow, and Katherine was looking forward to seeing them again. It was lonely in camp when they were gone.

On Monday morning, as the first glimmer of light rose over the trees, Katherine climbed out of bed shivering in the cold. She pulled on her long underwear and cotton stockings, and donned a warm flannel shirt and one of her two heavy winter skirts. She shoved her feet into her sturdy oxfords and then went out to stoke the fire.

With warmth emanating from the tiny heater that stood in the receiving area, Katherine made her way around the counter and into the bull pen, where the stock was on display. She straightened a row of neatly ordered tobacco containers and restacked the already neat flannel shirts. She counted the pencils and aligned the writing tablets, although they stood as straight as tin soldiers. She wiped dust from a dustless counter and then stood peeking out the window at the opening in the woods, where her girls would eventually appear.

Finally she wandered over to the cook shanty to find Luc and the cruiser with several others of the in-camp crew.

The jacks were already outside preparing for the big day. Katherine took a seat, helping herself to pancakes and sausage and listening to the men's talk. In time, she wandered back to the wanigan, trimmed the wick on the lamp, cleaned the chimney, and added oil. She stuffed a couple of logs into the heater, swept the floor, and checked the books. Then she stepped outside, peering into the darkened tunnel, where the trees arched over the two-track tote road. She stood still, watching and waiting.

At last Hannah and Willow burst from the forest, obviously engrossed in a world of their own. They broke into a run, racing toward the wanigan.

"Good morning, girls," Katherine called.

"Good morning," the girls responded in chorus. They whisked past Katherine and went inside, laughing and giggling all the way.

After a few hour-long minutes, Maggie and Faith Ann emerged from the forest with hands entwined.

Katherine reached out and Faith Ann began to run. The little girl flung herself at Katherine, squealing with joy. "I saw a deer in the woods, Mama. I saw a deer in the woods."

Katherine stooped, swept Faith Ann into her arms, and held her close, availing herself of a big hug and a kiss. "You saw a deer in the woods? How exciting!"

"Yeah, he was a great big deer, and he ran right out in front of us." Faith Ann's eyes sparkled. "But he ran away 'cause he was in a big hurry."

"And did you have a good time with Mrs. Maggie?"

"Oh yes, Mama. I got to ride Lulu, and I made a cake, and I fed the chickens, and I . . ."

"Well, it's good you had fun while you were there, but I'm glad you're home now, because I miss you when you're gone."

Faith Ann wriggled free and dashed inside. "I gotta get Ben. I forgot to take Ben, and he's lonely."

Katherine and Maggie followed Faith Ann into the wanigan. "Well, Maggie, how did it go?"

"It went fine, as always."

Katherine pulled the door closed. "I was sure it would." Maggie took a seat in the chair by the heater, as Faith Ann exploded back into the room. "Look, Mrs. Maggie, I found Ben. He was under the bed."

The little girl thrust her doll into Maggie's face. "He was lonesome, but he's better now 'cause we're here."

"Faith Ann," Katherine said, "don't interrupt when adults are talking."

Maggie just smiled and held the doll away from her face. "Well, hello Ben. It's nice you're feeling better."

"Aunt Mae made Ben for me 'cause Annie got losted in the ocean."

Katherine sighed. It seemed so long ago that they had set out in a rowboat to come across the lake to Michigan. Annie had flipped overboard and still lay somewhere at the bottom of that great expanse of water.

"That's too bad about Annie," Maggie responded. "I bet Ben's a lot of fun, though."

"Yeah, but I miss Annie. She c'd be Ben's sister." Faith Ann hugged Ben. "It's OK, though, 'cause she c'n play with

Johnny. Johnny went to be with Jesus, and he needed a dolly to play with."

Hannah and Willow came out from behind the privacy curtain. "Hey, Ma, look at this."

Willow dropped Grandmother Hamlin's brooch into her mother's hand. "It's an heirloom. Hannah got it from her Great Grandma."

Faith Ann leaned over Maggie's lap and thrust her face forward, obscuring the brooch that Maggie now held. "Someday I'm gonna get a brooch just like it."

Hannah bristled. "Oh no you won't, because you can't. You can't get an heirloom unless your grandma gives it to you. It has to come from someone in your family."

Faith Ann fell into a pout and Katherine stepped in. "Now, Hannah, be kind."

"Well, she can't."

Suddenly, the air reverberated with the scraping of wagon wheels, and everyone rushed outside to watch the tote wagon as it rolled into camp.

"Whoa there," tote teamster Joe Fossett hollered. "I said whoa, you sons of hell."

The rig squealed to a stop in front of Luc's office, and Joe climbed down flipping the reins over the buckboard and disappearing inside.

Photographer, Thomas Lind, climbed onto the whippletree and down to the ground. He turned and reached up for his equipment.

"Here, let me get that for you." Yuri Tomich, the county scaler, handed the camera and gear over the side to Tom. Then he, too, climbed down.

With the arrival of these two important men, the festivities could begin.

Clive walked toward the loading deck with Don Parker, the Waterhouse cruiser. They talked of their love for the forest—the great pines that whispered softly in the wind, the animals that flitted here and there in the underbrush, foliage that filled the senses with tranquility. Yes, Clive could see a future for himself as a cruiser, like his friend, exploring the land for profitable stands of timber.

"You know," he said, "someday I'd like to do some cruising myself."

"That's interesting," Don responded. "I have a team going to the Upper Peninsula next summer, and we need another compass man. Is that something that would interest you?"

A surge of pleasure skittered up Clive's spine. "Yes, I think I'd like that. Tell me more."

"There'll be five men, a cook, two compass men, and two appraisers. We'll be going into Canada for about six weeks."

"How soon do you need to know?"

"Soon. We're meeting at the Traverse Bay Hotel right after the logging season closes. The crew should be complete by that time."

Clive and Don approached the site for the contest and took their places near the loading deck with Luc, Tom Lind, and Yuri Tomich. Katherine and her girls stood nearby with the Nilssons.

Clive smiled. It pleased him to see the two families getting along well. He greeted Katherine with a nod and turned his attention to the loading.

Two skids had been propped against the sleigh bunk, and toploader, Boris Horowitz, stood on the bunk poised and ready. "Let 'er rip," he shouted, and the crew swung into motion.

The tailers-down rolled a log off the deck, the senders-up swung their canthooks, positioning the log at the base of the skidders.

The timber rolled into place, and the chainers flung a heavy chain over and around it.

"Giddap," yelled the teamster, and the horses plodded up the cross-haul. Up and up rolled the log on the skidders, dropping onto the sleigh-bunk, where Boris Horowitz swung his peavey and positioned it just right to balance the load. Then he turned.

"Tailer down," Boris yelled, and another immense log rolled off the deck. Senders-up maneuvered it into place, and chainers wrapped it for the haul upward.

"Lift," shouted the senders-up. "Giddap," yelled the teamster.

"Snort," went the horses, and the logs rolled up the skids in a steady succession.

All the while, Boris Horowitz danced over the load, leaping from log to log, rolling each one into place, and calling out indelicate directions to the rest of the crew. He did his job with skill and integrity, fitting each log exactly in place.

The load grew higher and higher—five feet . . . seven feet . . . eight feet. Tension mounted—ten feet . . . eleven feet . . . twelve feet. Everyone knew that a misadjusted log could cause the entire load to come crashing down with murderous possibilities for anyone nearby.

Finally, Boris pronounced the load complete. The chainers secured it with a final wrap, and three more logs were placed on top to pull the chain as tight as possible.

A loud cheer rang out from everyone present.

Thomas Lind positioned his camera, and the crew took their places on or near the load. Boris Horowitz stood straight and proud at the top along with Klause Bruner and Marvin Paulich. Chainers stood close at hand with tailers-down and senders-up.

"OK, hold your place," Lind called. He crawled under the camera's hood, held his hand high, and activated the shutter. The DuBois masterpiece was etched in history.

Slowly the horses moved along the ice road with the towering load gliding behind—twenty feet . . . fifty feet . . . eighty-seven feet.

And the camp exploded into clapping and shouting. It was a day for celebration.

Some time later, after the load was dismantled, Yuri Tomich would scale it for board-feet. Then Thomas Lind would take the measurement along with his picture into town. The reporter would write his story, and the DuBois crew's load would be emblazoned on the front page of the *Charlevoix Times*.

Hannah and Willow stood with several other locals watching Jules Bleecker, the blacksmith, as he fanned the coals in the fire pit. His face glowed red, and his muscles bulged as he reached for an iron rod.

Still pumping the bellows, he buried one end in the fire until it began to glow pink and then red. He lifted the rod from the fire, rested it on the anvil, and raised his heavy hammer. He let the hammer fall, mashing the glowing metal and forming it into an arc. He turned the emerging tool and struck it again, repeating the process until it lost its red glow and resisted his blows. Then he thrust it back into the fire for a second round. Jules heated and tapped and tapped and heated. And when the rod became a perfect hook with a sharp point on one end, he dipped it into a vat of cold water.

Spatter, sizzle, hiss. The iron sputtered its complaint as it lost its red color.

"Yep," Jules said. "I can make most any tool you might want. Just give me the iron, a good hot fire, and a hammer."

Hannah had seen enough. She and Willow wandered away. "Hey, Clive," she called as they stepped outside.

"Well, Hannah and Willow, how're you doing?"

"Good," Hannah said. "And you know what? I'm teaching Willow to cipher."

"Well, how about that."

"And it's easy," Willow said.

"I'm sure it is; you're a smart girl."

Clive turned to Don Parker. "Don, you remember Hannah and Willow. We talked to them this morning at the loading."

"Yes, of course I remember. How could I forget? It's not often I get to visit with two such fine looking young ladies, especially in the logging camp."

Hannah's heart surged with satisfaction. "Well, thank you, Mr. Parker."

Clive and the cruiser moved toward the barn and the girls fell into step, nearly running to keep up.

They stepped into the barn, and Henri LeBlanc, the barn boss, came to meet them. "Bon soir," he called. "C'est bon de te voir."

"Bon soir, Henri," Clive responded. "It's good to see you, too."

Henri smiled through a ragged beard that stuck out in all directions. A red bandana tied around his forehead was all that kept his hair from doing the same.

"Come," he said. He reached up and grabbed a lantern that hung from a wire stretched the full length of the barn, and hauled it along as he walked to provide light for his task.

Soon, Hannah's eyes grew accustomed to the shadowy interior of the barn, and she noted the stalls and the mangers made of small poles. She observed the harnesses hanging from the walls . . . and the traps and the logging chains and the shed-like area where oats and hay were stored. Most of the time, at Katherine's insistence, she avoided the men's buildings, but today was her chance to explore.

Finally, Hannah had had enough. She and Willow wandered out of the barn, leaving the men to their own activities.

"So what would you like to do next?" she asked her friend. "Oh, I don't know." Willow's voice trembled, and Hannah thought she seemed tired and a little drawn. "Are you OK?"

"I'm fine. Whatever you want to do is OK with me." "You want to go back to the wanigan?"

"No, I'm fine. Maybe we could get something to eat."

So the girls went to the cook shanty, where Emma supplied each of them with a tasty cinnamon roll and a cup of coffee.

Hannah wasn't crazy about coffee, but she sipped it slowly, pretending to love the stuff. Willow took a swallow and rested her head in her hands. Her face was dark with pain.

"Willow," Hannah said. "Do you have one of those headaches again? Have you told your ma about them yet?"

"No, I didn't tell her. There's nothing to be done about it."

"Well then, let's go to the wanigan, anyway."

"I can't do that. It'd scare the wits out of Ma."

"C'mon, this needs to be done. You've put it off too long as it is."

Hannah pushed her dishes away and took Willow's hand. Willow sighed and followed Hannah across the road, apparently in too much pain to resist.

141

As they entered the wanigan, Maggie took one look at her daughter and rushed to her side. "Willow, what's wrong?"

Hannah pulled back the privacy curtain and ushered Willow to the bunk. "She has a headache. She's been getting them for weeks and she promised to tell you about it, but she never did."

The color drained from Maggie's face as she hovered over her only child.

"Willow, why didn't you tell me? Here, let me get you some water. Katherine, what have you got for pain?"

Katherine stepped behind the counter and pulled out a bottle of Dr. Davis Pain Killer.

Maggie held the bottle to Willow's lips. "How long has this been going on, anyway? Why didn't you tell me?"

Willow didn't answer. She just lay on Katherine's bed with a cloth over her eyes, moaning softly.

In time, the pain eased, and Maggie decided to take her daughter home. So Jake hitched the horse to the jumper and they left camp.

That night, Hannah lay in her bunk thinking of Willow. What was the meaning of all those headaches? The young woman should see a doctor, but how could she? There were no doctors within thirty miles. What if Willow were really sick? Could she make it to town in time to save her life?

Chapter Nineteen

Several weeks had passed since the big contest, and Katherine had settled into the relentless grind of lumber camp life. Just now she sat in the camp office, leaning over her books. Hannah had gone to the Nilssons to help Willow with her ciphering, and Faith Ann played with Ben near the heater.

Willow's headaches had become worse, and Hannah often came home worried and upset. When Hannah suggested the girl go to the doctor in town, Willow insisted the headaches would get better. "And besides, we can't afford a doctor."

"God help that girl," Katherine whispered to herself.

Startled, she drew back. Was that a prayer? Certainly not! Katherine had better things to do than pray to an angry God who only did her harm. On the other hand, Sister Olivia had said God didn't cause harm. He only allowed it to happen. Maybe Katherine needed special tuning to grow strong for her mission in life. Did Katherine have a mission in life? As she sat pondering the matter, the door opened and Clive entered.

"Good morning, Katherine. How're things?"

Immediately, Faith Ann leaped to her feet, flinging herself at Clive's knees. "Mister Clive, you came to see me."

Clive looked down with a smile. "Yes, Faith Ann, I came to see you." He ruffled the little girl's curly brown locks and turned to Katherine. "Is Hannah around?"

Katherine bristled. Why was Clive always looking for Hannah? The two of them were forever going off by themselves, mumbling in tones that no one else could hear. Arithmetic or no arithmetic, Katherine didn't like it.

"Hannah's at the Nilssons'," she said, clipping her words. "She's helping Willow with her ciphering."

Clive stuffed his scotch cap into his pocket, brushing his hand over his hair to smooth it into place. "Well, I'll just have to go over there, I suppose."

He turned toward Katherine with a grin, "But in the meantime, what's going on with you?" He unbuttoned his mackinaw and pushed it back, resting his hands on his hips.

Katherine took a deep breath. Surely Clive wouldn't mess with her fourteen-year-old stepdaughter. "Actually, I'm looking forward to warm weather and going back to Hitchcock. I want to get started with my bakery business."

"Ahh, Katherine, what a fine woman you are," Clive said. "One of these days some lucky man'll come along and you'll remarry. I could almost wish it were me."

A rush of heat flooded Katherine's face, and she turned her back. Was he really suggesting they might develop a relationship? Surely not, although the thought had crossed Katherine's mind. After all, she'd once cared a great deal for Clive, and he was Faith Ann's father. But Clive didn't know that. His love was the woods, and Katherine wasn't about to be left at home alone while her man traipsed around in the wilderness.

"Let's go over to the cook shanty for coffee," she suggested. It was a good way to divert Clive's attention.

"Sure thing." Clive bent, swept Faith Ann into his arms, and headed outside.

As they entered the building, the aroma of fresh bread filled the air. Luc and Jasper sat at the table with Jake the handyman, drinking coffee, eating fresh rolls, and preparing for the day's work.

"Come sit," Jasper said, as they entered. "We have a little offering from one of the best cooks in these parts."

Emma appeared around the counter, grinning her thanks at her husband.

Katherine and Clive took seats on the bench, and Emma poured coffee. Then she filled a cup with milk for Faith Ann.

Faith Ann's face twisted into a pout. "I'm a big girl. I want coffee."

"Faith Ann, mind your manners." Katherine's face shot a warning. "You're not . . ."

Before Katherine could finish, Emma poured a splash of coffee into Faith Ann's glass. "There you go, young woman."

Faith Ann's dark eyes sparkled with joy. "I'm a big girl," she repeated. "I can drink coffee."

Katherine smiled. How could she say more, when every face in the room wore a satisfied grin?

But the merriment in the shanty was shattered in an instant. The door crashed open and Hannah fell through the opening, saucer-eyed and gasping for breath. "Katherine . . . you gotta . . . come . . . quick."

"Hannah!" Katherine threw her legs over the bench, bounding across the room to her daughter's side.

"Willow's sick. She's awful sick. She's got one of those headaches . . . and she's screaming . . . and hitting her head with her fists." Everyone in the room leaped to attention. Luc was halfway out the door shouting orders. "Jake, go tell Henri to get the wagon ready. Emma, you watch Faith Ann."

Faith Ann looked up at Katherine with pleading eyes. "I wanna go."

"No, Faith Ann, you can't go."

"C'mere, Faith Ann," Emma called. "Look what Auntie Emma has for you."

Emma led Faith Ann into the kitchen, and Katherine left the building with Hannah and Luc and Jasper.

Minutes later, after a gut-jarring ride through the woods, Jasper reined in the horses at Maggie's cabin. Almost before the wagon stopped, Hannah leaped over the side. Clive reached for Katherine, and she fell into his arms.

Entering the house, Katherine found Maggie sitting on Hannah's bed, rocking back and forth and moaning. Sabaka lay on the floor with her head beneath her paws. Dread hung in the air like yesterday's shroud.

Katherine moved near the bed and brushed Willow's face. The girl didn't move. Katherine felt for the girl's pulse and found none. She laid her hand on Willow's chest . . . still nothing. Maggie's daughter was dead.

Katherine turned to Maggie. "I'm so sorry."

A desperate sob echoed through the room, and Maggie collapsed onto Katherine's breast, wailing in agony. Hannah sat nearby with teary eyes. The men stood in stony silence with hats in hand.

After several long minutes, Luc spoke. "I think we should pray."

Katherine gave a start of surprise. Whoever heard of a lumber camp boss who prayed?

"God in heaven," Luc said, "receive this child into your arms. Comfort her mother and give her peace."

A long, reflective silence filled the room, and then Katherine and Hannah wrapped Willow's body in a blanket while the men helped Maggie onto the settee. The bereaved mother sat with shoulders trembling and chest heaving.

In time, Luc leaned toward Jasper, pulling his hat out of his pocket. "We better go back to camp and have Jake prepare a box for the body."

He pulled his hat over his head and turned toward the door. "We'll come back tomorrow for final rites and decide then what to do about Maggie."

"Hannah," Katherine said, "you go back and take care of Faith Ann tonight. I'll stay here with Maggie."

That night, Maggie lay in her bed crying until the wee hours. Katherine lay by her side, reviewing the events of the day.

Why God, why? What was it Sister Olivia had said? *Troubles come, but when they do, God sends His Spirit to help.* Was God's Spirit here now? If so, what was He doing to help? Katherine could see no sign of care or concern from God.

About mid-morning on the following day the wagon returned with most of the in-camp crew. A crude wooden box, hastily made out of weatherworn lumber, jostled in its bed.

Luc and Jasper lifted Willow's body and placed it in the coffin, taking care to keep it wrapped. The other men dug a shallow grave in the back yard. Then all those present gathered around the pall.

"God in heaven," Luc said, "we commit this child to You. Take her into Your presence and give her peace."

Willow's body was lowered into the grave, and the parting was done. At Katherine's invitation, Maggie chose to return with her to Camp DuBois.

Luc turned to his crew. "Jake, take Sabaka and the cow over to the Burchard farm. Ben'll take care of them, for a few days at least, until Maggie knows what she wants to do."

Before they left, Maggie wrote a note.

> *Dear Max,*
> *Willow got a terrible headache on Friday and died real fast. You'll find her grave in the back yard.*
> *I'm at Camp DuBois. You can come and get me there.*
>
> *Maggie*

Maggie moved through the next several days in a fog. She rose, dressed, and sat by the fire, rocking to and fro in a daze. She wandered around camp with addled eyes, focusing on nothing. At night she lay in bed crying. Katherine tried to comfort her friend, but Maggie seemed beyond her reach.

Then one day the rocking stopped. Maggie's head seemed to clear, and she looked around.

"I gotta go home," she said. "Max could come back any day now, and I want to be there when he does."

Katherine exited the bull pen, where she'd been tending camp supplies. "Are you sure?" she asked, looking into Maggie's eyes. Her friend appeared to be lucid at last.

"Yes, I'm sure." Maggie began to gather her belongings.

"What if I send Hannah with you for a few days? Then you wouldn't be alone."

"That would be nice, but I have to go home."

So Katherine and Maggie made their way to the cook shanty, where Hannah was helping Angus Muldoon with the dishes and Emma was baking bread.

"Maggie wants to go home," Katherine announced. "And I'd like to send Hannah with her."

Emma nodded. "She's doing better, huh?"

"Yes," Maggie said with finality in her voice. "And I think I should be home when Max comes."

"Well, I think it's a good idea to send Hannah along. Hannah, you go ahead and get your things."

"Mama, Mama." Faith Ann yanked on Katherine's skirt. "I wanna go, too. I can help."

Maggie's face lit up with joy at the little girl's plea. "I'd like that, Faith Ann."

Katherine hesitated but finally allowed the visit. She could hardly say no when both Maggie and Faith Ann seemed so pleased with the idea. Besides, it wasn't all bad to be left unencumbered at the end of the season while she closed down the wanigan.

"Camp closes in a few days," Hannah said as she and Faith Ann gathered supplies for the trip. "Why don't we just take all our things with us? Then when you're done here, you can pick us up over at Maggie's place and we'll go home from there."

The idea sounded reasonable to Katherine. "Good idea," she said. "You take your things with you and we'll be that much closer to closing down for summer."

Later that afternoon, Katherine stood with Luc, watching as Jake flicked the reins, and the wagon disappeared into the forest. "Luc," she said, when the wagon was out of sight, "where did you learn to oversee a burial like that?"

"Well, I guess you could say I learned it from my pa. Pa was an itinerant preacher, and we went to three different church services every Sunday."

Katherine fell back, startled. "Then how did you end up out here?"

Luc's smile took on a melancholy quality. "My pa died when I was fourteen. He was coming home from a meeting and was caught in a storm. They found him in the woods three days later."

Tears gathered behind Katherine's eyes. Tears for a fourteen-year-old boy who lost his father to an untimely death.

"I had to go to work to support the family," Luc continued, "so I got a job in the camps as a shanty boy. And I just came up through the ranks."

Over the following days, anticipation in the camp grew to a nearly overwhelming pitch. Some men grew loud, telling lewd stories of booze and women and wild adventure. Others, married jacks especially, drew inward, sharing pictures of family they'd tucked into watch caps or behind the metal backs of mirrors or into razor cases.

One night, Otto Krause entered the wanigan, his eyes etched with longing. "I need something for my family," he said.

Opening his pocket-watch, he held it out for Katherine to see. "The woman there is my wife, Bonnie, and those are my two kids, Kurt and Anna."

The young woman who looked out at Katherine wore a cheerful smile. Dark hair circled her face and fell softly around her shoulders. Beside her stood a boy who looked to be about four years old and a girl about seven.

"That's a fine looking family." Katherine said. "I suppose they're eager for you to come home."

"And I'm eager to go home."

Otto dropped the watch back into his pocket and scanned the shelves. "Bonnie says they're getting along OK, but I still worry."

After a long and careful perusal of the stock, Otto pointed. "Give me a nickel's worth of horehound for the kids and a pen and writing tablet for Bonnie."

Katherine supplied the requested items, and Otto stuffed them into his shirt as if they were diamonds to be protected with his life. Then he wandered back across the road to the men's quarters.

Other Jacks came into the wanigan with their sights on far less honorable pursuits. They bounded through the door, clean-shaven and sporting new haircuts, telling tales of drinking and brawling. As the excitement grew, the stories became increasingly more candid, sometimes filling Katherine's ears with things that would have been better left unsaid.

Katherine sighed. The men weren't the only ones who longed for the camp's closing. Hitchcock and her bakery called ever more loudly.

Clive walked briskly along the tote road toward Camp Mishkin. It was spring, and the rains had come. The snow had begun to melt, and the ground was wet and soggy. Runoff flowed into rivers, and the rivers were beginning to swell. Before long, the log drives would begin. Great mountains of logs would be thrust into the current and sent thundering downriver to the booming grounds. There they would be sorted by log-marks and sluiced into holding ponds to await transformation into huge stockpiles of pine lumber.

Camps were stocking river wanigans with food, medicine, and other necessities. River-hogs were spinning tales of logjams, jam crackers, and territorial battles with farmers—and death at the hands of an angry crush of logs. The river-hog's job was hazardous and demanding, but the challenge and the very danger itself seemed to draw these men like a magnet.

Clive had plans for the summer as well. He had signed on with Don Parker to cruise the Upper Peninsula for Waterhouse Lumber. Clive looked forward to long summer nights in the forest he loved, exploring the territory seeking new stands of timber.

CHAPTER TWENTY

Hannah lifted the water pail from Maggie's washstand and headed out the back door. She passed Willow's grave with its dark, freshly dug soil, hardly noticing the large rock at one end. She hurried up the path, avoiding the puddles that were everywhere this time of year and came to a shallow ditch, where an old iron pipe angled upward from the earth, spouting water onto the ground.

She slid the pail under the pipe, waited for it to fill, and headed back to the cabin. There she found Maggie, rummaging through an old crate.

"There are bulbs in here somewhere," Maggie said. "Willow always loved spring flowers, and I'm going to plant crocus and daffodils on her grave."

Hannah set the pail on the washstand, dipped the long-handled dipper into the water, and handed it to Faith Ann. Faith Ann drank her fill and handed the dipper back to Hannah, who helped herself and then hung the dipper on the nail.

"Here they are," Maggie said. She lifted an old bag, soiled by its earthy contents and bulging with tiny sprouts. "Come on, girls. Let's plant flowers."

Shoulders bent, Maggie led the way across the backyard toward Willow's grave.

Nearing the knoll where Willow lay, Hannah noticed a large rock with words hand painted on it: *Willowbelle Nilsson, 1883–1897, The Daughter of My Heart.*

Maggie must have seen it, too, for tears began to spill over her cheeks. "Max was here," she whispered. She fell on her knees, digging in the cold, dark soil. "He was here, and he didn't come for me."

Tears dropped soundlessly onto the ground, as the twice-bereaved woman worked the dark, moist soil.

Hannah stood silent for several long minutes, watching and wondering what to do. Then she took Faith Ann by the hand, and the two girls went inside.

Later that night, after Faith Ann had been tucked into Maggie's bed, Hannah sat on the settee with Sabaka's head in her lap. Only the crunching of the corn-husk tick disturbed the silence.

"Mrs. Maggie," she said at last, "what will you do now?" Maggie took in a deep breath and let it out slowly, apparently considering the thought. "I don't rightly know."

The older woman fingered the hem of her apron. "Maybe I'll just stay here. Max might come back, you know."

"But the camps are closing. The tote wagons won't be going by, like they are now. You'll be alone with no way of getting out."

"Well, I can get Lulu and Sabaka, and I know the woods."

A wistful smile covered Maggie's face. "I know where the berry patches are and how to raise a garden from last year's harvest. I can even fish and shoot a rabbit if I need to."

"But, Mrs. Maggie, you've had Willow to keep you company. Now you're alone."

"I've faced difficulty before, and I can do it again."

A burst of anger coursed through Hannah's veins. Who did Max Nilsson think he was? He had no right to treat Mrs. Maggie this way. He was a heartless old beast with no thought for anybody but himself.

"Mrs. Maggie," Hannah said, murmuring into the stillness, "maybe you could move to Hitchcock, where there are people to help you when you need it."

"I'll be all right," Maggie responded. "I may go back to my parents' farm. Then I wouldn't be alone."

Maggie rose, laid her apron over a chair, and let the curtains down over the windows. "I think I'll turn in."

Hannah slid from under Sabaka's head, made her way into Willow's bedroom, and crawled into her friend's bed.

Maggie lifted the lamp and carried it into her own room. Soon the cabin descended into darkness.

Several days later, Hannah sat at the table ciphering, while Maggie and Faith Ann sat on the settee looking at pictures.

"This is my ma standing by the chicken coop," Maggie said. "And that's Paradise Lake behind her."

Faith Ann almost danced with glee. "Mrs. Maggie, what is it like where you came from?"

"Oh, Faith Ann, Paradise Lake is a beautiful place way up north, where the water's so cool and clear you can see almost to the bottom of the lake. I used to sit in my pa's boat and fish and dream of castles and mansions and heavenly places."

A smile unlike any Hannah had ever seen covered Maggie's face.

"My ma and pa moved there when I was just a little girl. They were planning to go farther out west, but the land was so beautiful they decided to stay. They claimed seventy-five acres and have lived there ever since."

"Could I go swimming in Paradise Lake?"

"I guess you could if you wanted to. Mostly, we just farmed and fished and hunted."

Maggie held up another photograph. "And this is a picture of my pa and me with the bass we caught in the cove. My pa knew right where all the best fishing spots were."

Hannah gave up ciphering and took a seat on the settee.

"And here's a picture of me with my ma and pa standing near the Ojibwa trail."

Maggie handed Hannah a picture of a log house with two big maple trees in the front yard and a lake behind. "That's our house. I was twelve years old when that picture was taken."

Hannah sat with Maggie and Faith Ann, looking at pictures until the box was empty. Then Maggie placed the pictures back in the box and put it on a shelf. A wistful smile spread across her face. "Maybe someday I'll go back there."

Later, Hannah lay abed, pondering the twists and turns of life. Maggie and Faith Ann were inseparable these days. They walked in the woods and picked pussy willows and pored over

Maggie's scrapbook. They baked gingerbread men and cooked squirrel pie from canned meat that Maggie had in the cellar. They played I-spy and hide-the-thimble and I'm-hiding-I'm-hiding. Once Maggie chose the box with pictures of her folks' cabin as an imaginary hiding place, and Hannah had to help Faith Ann to ask the right questions to find her.

As Hannah lay reviewing the day's events, an eerie feeling of discomfort slithered into her bones. Her breath quickened and her heart beat fast, as if her world were about to collapse. She pushed the feeling aside, but it kept filtering back into her consciousness. Finally, a curtain of dreams fell and Hannah drifted into sleep.

Camp DuBois had come to the end of its season. Katherine had worked half the night preparing time checks for the jacks. The teamsters loaded their sleighs with blankets and hay and harnesses. They gathered tools that needed repair and gear of every sort and climbed aboard their sleighs to begin the long trek down the slushy trail toward town. Most of the other men left on foot about ten o'clock in the morning, carrying their turkeys and hoping to reach town by the next day.

At about noon, Klause finished hauling sleighs up onto skids for storage and left for Camp Rifkin with Jasper and Emma. Katherine still had accounting to do, and she and Luc would leave in the morning on the tote wagon. They would swing by Maggie's place to pick up the girls and then be on their way home. Camp DuBois felt lonely and deserted.

As Katherine finished packing leftover items from the bull pen, the sound of snorting horses and creaking wagon wheels announced the arrival of Ivan Belofsky, the summer watchman. The wagon slowed to a stop, and Ivan hopped over the side with his turkey. He slung the bag over his shoulder and approached Luc.

"I've cleaned out the office," Luc said. "We'll let you get settled, and then you and I can take a trip through the camp before Katherine and I head out."

Ivan walked with Luc toward the office, where he would spend the summer months. He seemed to be looking forward to the warm season with its long days and empty nights. It took a special kind of person to serve as camp watchman.

Soon, Luc and Ivan went to the woods to inspect the camp. Katherine and Joe loaded the few remaining supplies onto the tote wagon. Then when Luc returned, he and Katherine climbed aboard the tote wagon, Joe Fossett flicked the reins, and the wagon rumbled down the road on its way to a different world. Katherine was, at last, on her way to life in Hitchcock and the realization of her dream. She'd call her bakery Katie's Place.

But first, she must provide a proper burial for Frank's body. A knife pierced her heart as she considered the task and the pain of her husband's loss that it would surely bring. This was not the way she'd planned to spend her life.

CHAPTER TWENTY-ONE

A dull haze hovered over the earth as the tote wagon lumbered through the mud and slush that overspread the forest floor in spring. Katherine leaned first one way and then the other, in harmony with the slope of the earth under the wagon wheels. Maggie's cabin was just ahead, and they'd pick up the girls. Then they'd be on their way to Hitchcock and a new life. Katherine would start her bakery, and Hannah and Faith Ann would have the things they needed to live well. She had promised Frank, and she intended to keep that promise.

The wagon came upon a giant mud hole that blocked the entire roadway, but Joe Fossett didn't flinch. He simply flicked the reins, turned the horses into the woods, and slogged around the wallow, lumbering back onto the two-track route toward town. Later, the wagon rolled into a swampy bog where logs had been placed across the passage to build a corduroy road. Joe urged the horses forward, clobbering over the logs until Katherine thought she surely must turn to butter.

"Hey, look," Joe called as they crested a rise in the trail. "Someone's coming this way."

Katherine peered down the tree-sheltered path at a figure that appeared to be a young woman. The figure paused as though gasping for breath, and then raced on.

Hannah! It was Hannah!

Coming within reach, Hannah flung herself against the wagon in one giant leap.

"Katherine," she cried, "I didn't mean it. It just happened, and I couldn't help it . . .because I didn't know."

"Hannah, what's going on? You couldn't help what? And where's Faith Ann?"

"Faith Ann's gone. I didn't mean it; it just happened."

Fear exploded in Katherine's chest. "Hannah, what are you saying?"

"Maggie took Faith Ann. I woke up this morning, and they were gone. My case was open, and stuff was strewn all over the place. And they were nowhere around."

Katherine's mind reeled. This couldn't be true.

"I looked everywhere. They're not in the house; they're not outside; they're not anywhere!"

"C'mon, Joe," Luc hollered. The two men leaped onto the ground, lifted Hannah by the waist, and fairly threw her over the side of the wagon. Soon they were racing pell-mell down the road toward Maggie's cabin.

"I knew something was wrong! I just knew it." Hannah cried as if her heart would break. "I had this awful feeling in the night—like something terrible was about to happen. It's my fault. I should have watched."

Katherine's emotions shouted an accusation—Then why didn't you watch?—But she knew it was a foolish thought. She swallowed her frustration and put an arm around Hannah's shoulder.

"It's OK, Hannah, it's OK. You couldn't have watched all night, especially when you didn't know for sure." Katherine hoped Hannah couldn't feel her resentment.

Soon the wagon drew to a stop at the Nilssons' cabin, where the men searched the grounds.

Katherine and Hannah entered the house and began to gather Hannah's things from the bedroom floor.

"Hannah," Katherine probed, do you remember anything? Anything that would give us a hint?"

"All I know is that I felt like something was wrong and I couldn't tell what it was."

Katherine looked through kitchen cupboards and drawers for papers. She searched the dining area for a note that might have been dropped. She looked in Maggie's bureau for any clue to the disappearance. But there was nothing—nothing that would give a hint about the direction Maggie might have taken.

Suddenly, Hannah burst into the kitchen, frustration and anger flaming in her eyes. "Grandmother Hamlin's brooch is gone," she yelled. "They stole my heirloom. Faith Ann knew better, but she took my heirloom."

"Now, Hannah, don't go jumping to conclusions. Let me take another look."

Katherine searched the bedroom again. She looked under the bed; she looked behind the chest of drawers and on the shelf above the nails where the clothing was hung. But the brooch was nowhere to be found. It did appear that Faith Ann had taken the heirloom with her, wherever she had gone.

Hannah began to fester. "Not only did she run away in the night, but she took my brooch. How dare she take my brooch?"

Katherine had no answer. No matter how much she wished it were different, it did appear that Maggie and Faith Ann had run off in the night with Hannah's heirloom. She rankled at the gall of the woman she had called friend. Katherine had gone out of her way to help Maggie, even sharing her bed, when Willowbelle died. And now the woman had stolen Katherine's child and Hannah's heirloom.

Anger and frustration boiled in Katherine's veins—anger at Maggie for running away, frustration at Hannah for letting it happen, and resentment at God for not controlling the situation. And though Katherine knew Faith Ann's disappearance was not Hannah's fault, she couldn't help feeling a sense of umbrage. She had trusted Hannah to watch the child. How could the girl have lost her little sister?

For several days, Luc and Joe tramped through the woods, but no sign of Maggie or Faith Ann ever turned up. It soon became clear that Maggie had struck out deliberately for some unknown location.

With a heavy heart, Katherine agreed to leave the forest. She and Luc and Hannah would go to Boyne City to report the disappearance to the constable.

The next day, Katherine sat in the Boyne City Police station, drumming her fingers on the arm of her chair. Hannah sat nearby with her chin glued to her chest.

"Mr. Payne will see you in a minute," the clerk had said. That was twenty minutes ago.

"Hannah, don't feel bad. You're not to blame. You know you couldn't stay awake all night." Even as Katherine spoke the words, her inmost being nurtured a sense of offense that nagged at her soul.

"Katherine's right," Luc whispered. "Don't blame yourself. It's just one of those things."

But Hannah continued to sit and brood, as if lost in a world of misery and shame.

Finally a preoccupied-looking Sheriff Neal Payne ambled into the room, potbelly hanging over his trousers and red plaid shirt open at the neck. He took a seat behind a big oak desk, nodding his balding head as he spoke.

"Now, Mrs. . . . Who did you say you are?"

"I'm Mrs. Katherine McLean, and my daughter is missing."

"Yes, now tell me how the whole thing happened."

The sheriff doodled while Katherine and Hannah related the events of the last several days. "Mm hmmm," he said as he scribbled. "I see . . . uh-huh."

"So you see, Sheriff Payne," Katherine said at last. "Mrs. Nilsson is somewhere in those woods with our baby, and we've got to find her."

The sheriff looked up with eyes remote and unresponsive. "Well, Mrs. McLean." He breathed deeply. "I'd like to tell you we'd bring your daughter back to you soon, but the truth of the matter is that people can vanish in those woods and never be seen again."

The sheriff handed Katherine a paper. "Here's a missing person's report. Fill it out, and my deputy and I will do what we can. But the chances your daughter will be found are not very good."

Katherine took the form, squinting at it through her tears. Name of missing person: Faith Ann McLean. Age: four years. Last seen: in the forest north of Hitchcock. Katherine's hands trembled so badly she could hardly write.

When she finally handed the paper to the deputy, tearstained and besmudged, her heart felt as if it had shriveled to a pea-sized mass of jelly.

"Thank you, Mrs. McLean," the deputy said. "We'll let you know if we find anything."

He laid the report atop a pile of papers on his desk and sat looking at the clock. It was almost quitting time, and he thumped his pencil in nervous agitation.

Katherine walked toward the door where Luc and Hannah waited. Fear and anger wrestled in her bones.

Hannah lay weeping in a hotel room at the Boyne City Inn. Katherine hated her; she could tell by the silence that hung between them. Hannah had known something was wrong, yet she slept through the night and let Maggie run away with Faith Ann. She didn't deserve to be loved.

Silently, she rose, dressed, and stepped out the door. She wandered aimlessly down the darkened street, wishing she could relive that awful night. She'd do it differently this time. She'd stay awake if it killed her.

She walked along the brick roadway with only the dim streetlamps to light her route. Shadows danced here and there in alleys and doorways, creating a sense of foreboding. She thought of what Sheriff Payne had said: People can vanish in those woods and never be seen again.

What if Hannah were to vanish without a trace? Would anyone care? In time, she came to the end of the street and turned onto a crossroad, walking mindlessly into the night, until she came to a cluster of small shops. She spotted a bench in front of a store and plopped down on it. *Hampton's Bakery,* the sign in the window read. Would there ever be a McLean's Bakery? Hannah doubted it. Katherine would never trust her with anything again.

Hannah sat on the bench, weeping until it seemed her soul would shrink into oblivion. Finally she rose, headed back to the hotel, and entered, hoping no one would notice her arrival. She crawled into bed, wishing she had the courage to disappear into the night. Tomorrow she and Katherine would take the train back to Hitchcock, where they'd have to tell Uncle Ned and

CHAPTER TWENTY-ONE

Aunt Mae about Faith Ann's disappearance . . . and Hannah's
carelessness.

Several weeks later, Katherine sat in the parlor, darning
socks with Aunt Mae. No word had come from Boyne City
regarding Faith Ann, and she had little hope of ever seeing her
daughter again.

"The sheriff is right," Uncle Ned had said. "People can
disappear in those woods. There's no way a man could secure
them all."

Katherine had thought several times about starting her
bakery, but she couldn't seem to develop any enthusiasm for the
project. She'd retrieved Frank's body from the icehouse and
given him a proper burial, but the permanence of the act only
increased her pain.

"I'm sorry, Frank," she'd whispered as she stood over the
grave. "I didn't keep my promise. I lost your baby, and I can't
find her." She fell on her knees, her body wracked with grief.

The atmosphere between Katherine and Hannah was fraught
with tension. The very sight of her stepdaughter filled Katherine
with pain. Sometimes she deliberately turned away so she
wouldn't have to look at the girl.

Then one night Katherine saw Maggie and Faith Ann in a
dream. They were walking down a forest path, picking berries
and eating them. Katherine ran to catch up to her child, but just
as she drew near, Maggie and Faith Ann disappeared. Again
and again, Katherine ran after her baby. Again and again, Faith
Ann disappeared.

"Faith Ann," she'd called. "Faith Ann, it's your mama. I'm
coming." Katherine's own voice jarred her into wakefulness.
She rolled over, crying into her pillow.

Who did Maggie think she was? She had no right to run off
with Katherine's child in the middle of the night. Katherine had
sent her girls to keep Maggie from feeling lonely, and this was
how Maggie repaid her. Maggie was nothing but a selfish old
woman who didn't care about anyone but herself.

And what kind of lawman was that Sheriff Payne anyway, sitting on his duff while her baby was lost? Sheriff Payne was nothing but a "pain" in the neck. And Hannah . . . why couldn't Maggie have taken Hannah instead of Faith Ann? Hannah was closer to Willow's age, and Hannah had been a problem ever since Katherine married Frank.

Katherine lay nursing her resentment. She resented Hannah for her unresponsiveness. She resented the fact that the girl had lain sleeping while Faith Ann was being stolen. She resented Hannah because Frank was gone and Katherine still had to have his bothersome teenage daughter around. Why couldn't Hannah just die and leave Katherine alone?

A sledge fell on Katherine's chest. She sat up, stunned at her own emotions. What sort of person resented someone just for being alive? Sister Olivia said God allowed pain to help people build character. Maybe Katherine needed character building.

"God, help me," Katherine cried. "I don't want to hate Hannah. I don't want to hate anyone. Please take this hate and resentment from my heart."

She buried her face in her pillow. "And help me to love Hannah. Hannah's all I have left. Help me to love her."

At once, a blanket of tranquility settled over Katherine's spirit. She might not start a bakery. She might not even find Faith Ann. But Katherine had peace in her heart and soul. She would survive.

CHAPTER TWENTY-TWO

The next afternoon, Katherine and Hannah walked down the lane toward Brown Lake. Katherine's mind was awhirl. She wanted to reach out to the girl she'd resented for so many weeks. She wanted to tell Hannah that her heart had been changed, that God had given her a new perspective on life.

"Do you ever think about the bakery we were going to start?" she asked, trying to begin a conversation.

"Sometimes."

Katherine steeled herself and tried again. "Isn't this a beautiful day with the trees budding and everything turning green?"

"Uh-huh."

The wall between them seemed impassable. As Hannah walked on she wore the same forlorn expression she'd worn constantly since Faith Ann's disappearance.

Katherine took a deep breath. It was obvious she was going to have to be more direct.

"Hannah, I want to talk to you. I know I've been hard to live with these last few weeks, and I'm sorry. We trusted Maggie. If we hadn't, I wouldn't have sent you girls over there."

Silence.

Katherine plunged forward. "Don't blame yourself, Hannah. You and I are all we have left. We have to work together, or we're lost."

Hannah stopped. She looked at Katherine with empty eyes and said nothing.

"I'm sorry for the way I've treated you," Katherine went on. "Can't we put the past behind us? Let's work together to be a family, even if there are only two of us."

Hannah's eyes were awash with tears. "I knew something was wrong," she cried. "I knew something was wrong, and I didn't do anything to stop it."

"Hannah, you're not to blame. I prayed to God last night, and He gave me peace. He can do the same for you . . . and then we can build a future together."

But Hannah was resolute; she would not forgive herself. Finally, Katherine left the matter with God. She'd done her best, and God must complete the work. Katherine was comforted knowing that if God could bring peace to her own heart, He could surely meet Hannah's need as well. Katherine would not give up. She'd pray until Hannah's need was met.

"C'mon, she said. "Let's go back to the house."

Clive leaned against his pillow at the Traverse Bay Hotel, hands behind his head and eyes wandering over the flowered paper on the wall. He wondered about Katherine and her girls. They should be in Hitchcock by now. Had Katherine begun preparations for her bakery? Was Hannah continuing to practice her ciphering? And how about Faith Ann? Was her smile as big as ever? Was she still the precocious little snippet that had so captured his heart—always assuring everyone that she was a big girl?

He decided he'd stop to see them when his stint in the north woods was over. He thought about Ontario and his first date with Katherine at the Dominion Day fireworks. They'd sat together on the hillside overlooking Lake Huron with the fireworks filling the sky and *ooohs* and *aaahs* reverberating on the air. Katherine had been so close, and Clive had been so captivated. Late in the evening, he'd taken advantage of the darkness to pull her close and kiss her. That was the beginning of a relationship he'd thought might last forever.

But then he'd gone to the lumber camp, and she'd vanished from his world.

What a surprise it had been when he found her in Hitchcock's General Store. She was as beautiful as ever, and his heart nearly leaped out of his chest at the sight of her.

Then, when she showed up at Camp DuBois with Frank McLean, he could hardly believe his eyes. He liked Frank and Hannah, and he adored little Faith Ann. Clive sighed and laid the memory aside. He had an appointment in the dining room, and he'd better be getting started.

As Clive stepped through the door and into the grand dining room, he hesitated, viewing his surroundings. Looking beyond the elegant golden draperies that flowed from ceiling to floor, he could see Grand Traverse Bay lapping at the shore. Strains of "Little Boy Blue" wafted on the air as the music man plied the grand piano in the corner.

Clive made his way across the room to where Don Parker sat with three other men.

"Clive, I'd like you to meet the men we'll be cruising with this summer," Don said as he approached. "Boris here will be cooking for us."

Don motioned toward a short, stout man with a balding hairline and smiling eyes. "And Anton and Der will appraise the lumber." The tall, lean man at the back of the table and his shorter but fleshier companion both smiled and nodded.

Clive returned the greeting and took a seat near the wall.

A young woman appeared at tableside with a pad in her hands. "Are you men ready to order?" She pulled a pencil from her apron pocket, looking straight at Clive. "We have turkey or pot roast tonight. Turkey is sixty-five cents and pot roast is seventy-eight cents."

"I'll have the pot roast," Clive responded.

The waitress took Clive's order and turned to the others. All ordered pot roast.

"Now then," Don said, as the waitress left. He pulled a map from his case and ran his finger across its northern border.

"We've got two and a half weeks before we leave, and there are some things we'll need to deal with before we go."

After much discussion about the upcoming assignment, Anton called the meeting to a close. "We'll get together here in two weeks," he said. "We won't be able to hang around, so be sure to be here. If you're late, we'll be forced to go without you."

The meeting was adjourned, and Clive left the hotel. He ambled across the lawn toward the beach, considering his options. He had fourteen days before he needed to meet with Don and the crew. That should be enough time to visit Katherine and her girls in Hitchcock.

Hannah sat on her bed in the pantry, looking out at Uncle Ned's barn, unpainted and weather-worn. A pathway led past it toward the little watershed called Brown Lake. Uncle Ned had said Brown Lake was so full of fish that people got bitten if they tried to swim in the water. Hannah smiled, wondering what it was like to be bitten by a fish.

Katherine had been as sweet as sugar ever since the afternoon they walked together down that path. She had said many times that Hannah was not to blame for Faith Ann's kidnapping, but Hannah wasn't so sure. Hannah was there that night, and she had known something was wrong. She'd felt the danger, and yet she slept.

How Hannah wished she'd never left Grandma and Grandpa McLean's house in Ontario. What were they doing? Were they well? She reached for her case and fingered through it to find the envelope of pictures she'd brought from Bounding so long ago. She thumbed through its contents. There was a picture of Grandma and Grandpa McLean, sitting on the porch, watching the fields for deer that so often ran across. And there was Seth, standing on the Lake Huron shoreline with Johnny in his arms. It felt like only yesterday that Hannah had run along that shore with her brother. Pictures were like that. They could make you feel so close to the past.

Hannah leaped to her feet. She knew where Faith Ann and Maggie were. They'd been looking at pictures the night before they disappeared. One of them showed Maggie's mother standing by the chicken coop with Paradise Lake behind her. Faith Ann had said she wanted to swim in that lake. They'd gone to Maggie's childhood home; Hannah was sure of it. She rushed from the pantry and into the sitting room where Katherine and Uncle Ned sat playing checkers.

"Katherine, I know where Faith Ann is! I know where she is!"

Katherine jumped to her feet, sending checkers flying all over the board.

"Faith Ann's up north at a little place called Paradise Lake." Hannah spewed information so fast she stumbled over the words. "I was trying to cipher, but I couldn't because they were looking at pictures."

"Hannah, slow down. I can't follow you."

"I know where Faith Ann is. She's at Maggie's folks' farm. I know where she is!"

"Are you sure? What makes you think so?"

"They were looking at pictures, and Faith Ann said she wanted to go up there."

Uncle Ned leaned forward. "And where is Maggie's parents' farm?"

"It's at Paradise Lake. She had a picture of her ma with Paradise Lake behind her."

Aunt Mae came bustling into the room. "What's all the commotion? I can hear you sputtering all the way out in the kitchen."

"Aunt Mae, listen." Hannah flew to Aunt Mae's side. "Maggie and Faith Ann—they're at Maggie's folks' place—at Paradise Lake."

"I was in the pantry looking at pictures of Grandma and Grandpa McLean and Seth. I was thinking of what it was like back there, and all of a sudden I remembered what Maggie said. She said she wanted to go home to Paradise Lake."

"So you think they've gone up north," Aunt Mae said.

"Yes. That's why I felt so uncomfortable the night before they left. It's gotta be where she's at."

Katherine's eyes grew bold and intense. "And if you're right, we should be able to go right up there and bring Faith Ann home."

"Now don't go jumping into things." Aunt Mae's face grew troubled. "Go to the sheriff and let him do the hunting."

"I already went to the sheriff, and he's about as useless as last year's potato peelings."

Uncle Ned stroked his balding head. "It could be harder than you think. That's unsettled territory up there."

"We'll take the train to a place Luc used to talk about called Hopewell. And then we'll hire a wagon to take us on up north. There's no way I could even think of staying here if there's a chance of finding Faith Ann."

Hannah could see that nothing would stop Katherine from going after her baby.

And nothing would stop Hannah from going along. Maybe she could undo the harm she'd done.

Katherine tucked all the money she had into a little pocket she'd sewn to the inside of her waistband in preparation for a trip north.

"You could go over to Boyne City and have the sheriff handle this," Aunt Mae said for the umpteenth time. "He's the one's supposed to deal with such things."

"And what good would that do? He already showed how much interest he has in the matter. And besides, his authority ends at the county boundary."

Katherine stuffed some underwear into a pillowcase, along with several pair of stockings, a comb, and a small, oval-shaped mirror with a wire hook on the back. She'd wash her dress the night before she left Hopewell, and it should do until she got to Paradise Lake.

Uncle Ned and Aunt Mae argued against the idea, but Katherine was not to be deterred, and in the end Aunt Mae loaned them her case to carry with them.

"Now you be careful," Aunt Mae said at last.

CHAPTER TWENTY-TWO

"Don't get yourselves killed on this crazy trip," Uncle Ned admonished.

Katherine and Hannah waited beside the tracks until the train came along. Then they picked up Aunt Mae's case and climbed aboard. "We'll be careful," Katherine promised. "And we'll be back soon."

"With Faith Ann," Hannah called.

CHAPTER TWENTY-THREE

Spring warmth filled the air as Clive walked through the forest toward Hitchcock. Trees were leafing out, decorating the world in various shades of green. Spring beauty, adders tongue, and Dutchman's breeches dotted the woodland floor, and small animals skittered about in the underbrush.

"My Bonnie lies over the ocean." Clive's heart sang as he exited the forest at Birch Lake Road.

"My Bonnie lies over the sea." He could hardly wait to see the look on Katherine's face when she opened the door to find him standing there. "Oh, bring back my Bonnie to me."

He passed the old Beasley place, where Katherine had once lived, rounded the corner at Kubek's blacksmith shop, and turned right onto Main Street. There he broke into a run, bounding across the porch at Hitchcock's General Store.

"G'morning Sam," he called.

"Well Clive Isaman, you old bushwhacker, what're you doing out here at this time of year?"

"Sam, do you remember the woman I met in here last fall?" "Yep, name's Katherine, Katherine McLean."

"Well, I'd like to visit her family, before I go north on a cruising assignment this summer. Got any idea where she is?"

"Not really. She was staying out at Ned McLean's place, but some woman kidnapped Faith Ann, and Katherine went after her."

"What? Someone stole Faith Ann?" Clive gaped in bewilderment. "Who? Where is she? How long has she been gone?"

"I heard it was someone from out by that camp where she worked—Maggie, I think they said her name was."

"Maggie! Maggie stole Faith Ann? Why would Maggie steal Faith Ann?"

"I heard the woman's daughter died, and she took Faith Ann as a replacement."

"Willow died?"

Disbelief clouded Clive's thinking. It seemed as if the world had fallen apart since he last saw Katherine.

"That's everything I know," Sam said. "You'll have to talk to Ned to get the particulars."

"Well, where can I find him?"

Sam walked around the counter and led the way out the front door. "Just head out of town past the church." He pointed west. "Go around Parson's Dome to the first long lane going south. That's Ned's lane. You can't miss it."

"Thanks, Sam."

Clive nearly flew off the porch, striding down the road at a near trot. Twenty minutes later he stood on Ned McLean's porch.

"Yes?" A petite older woman about fifty-five years old with salt-and-pepper gray hair answered the door. She looked up at Clive with expectant eyes.

"Hello, is this the McLean house?"

"Yes it is. I'm Mrs. McLean. What can I do for you?"

Just then a rangy-looking man came striding into the room with thumbs tucked under his suspenders, and stood behind the woman. "And who might you be?"

"Name's Clive Isaman, I'm looking for Katherine McLean, and I heard she was staying with you."

"That's right; she was. But she and Hannah took off on the train two days ago looking for Katherine's youngest daughter."

"Yes, that's what I heard. And what do you know about Faith Ann? Sam Hitchcock said she'd been kidnapped."

Ned McLean told Clive all he knew about Faith Ann and the kidnapping. "Hannah seems to think this Maggie woman took

Faith Ann up north to Paradise Lake where her folks live, so Katherine and Hannah headed north on the train a few days ago. We tried to talk 'em out of it, but Katherine was having nothing other than to go after her child."

"So how do they expect to get to Paradise Lake? The train doesn't go to Paradise Lake."

"They're planning to hire a wagon in Hopewell to go the rest of the way."

"Hopewell!" Clive didn't want to believe what he'd heard. "They can't get a wagon in Hopewell. Hopewell is nothing but an old lumber camp. There's a caretaker and his wife there, and the only way out is by train or boat. And neither will take them to Paradise Lake."

Ned McLean let out a long, slow breath. "Well, I doubt if Katherine'll come back here. She'll walk if she has to. She means to find that baby."

"Then I'm going after them."

"Well, we certainly won't try to stop you. It'd give us considerable comfort to know you were there."

Ned McLean dropped back a step. "But the train doesn't go through until tomorrow. Why don't you stay with us until then?"

"Thanks. That's very kind of you. I'll do just that."

That afternoon Clive sat on a cot in Ned McLean's pantry, writing a letter to Don Parker.

> *Dear Don,*
> *I've been caught in an emergency situation. I won't be back to leave with the team, so go on without me. Maybe I can do it another time.*
>
> *Clive*

Clive mailed the letter, and two days later he caught the train to Hopewell. God only knew what kind of trouble Katherine and Hannah might have fallen into on this unfathomable mission.

Katherine stood by the tracks with Aunt Mae's case in hand and her heart pounding. Beside her stood Hannah, gaping through saucer eyes. Hopewell was nothing but an empty, rundown old lumber camp.

"So, what do we do now?" Hannah asked.

"I don't know." Katherine breathed the words almost inaudibly.

Just then a wizened, older man came out of the barn, walking toward them with a tired, unsteady gait. His heavy brow and leathery skin bespoke many years of rough, outdoor living.

"Well, how-do, Ma'am," he said. "What brings two such fine looking ladies to Hopewell?"

Katherine took a deep breath and rushed forward. "Actually, we thought Hopewell was a town, and we were planning to hire a wagon to take us to Paradise Lake. I don't suppose you have a wagon for hire."

"We ain't got no wagon here. Best we can do is a boat to Lake Huron."

Katherine fought the tears that stung the back of her eyes and threatened to overflow her cheeks.

"My little daughter was stolen in the middle of the night," she said, "and we think her abductor came this way."

The man's eyes widened with concern. "Oh my, you must be just about crazy with worry!"

"Well, we're doing everything we can to find her."

"Come along and meet my wife; we'll see what we can do for you."

The man lifted Aunt Mae's case and led the way toward one of the camp buildings. "By the way, the name's Neal Bannister and my wife is Cory."

Katherine followed Neal Bannister toward what must have been the cook shanty when the camp was new. Inside, however, the long bench-lined camp tables that once filled the room had been replaced by a smaller dining set along the north wall. A handcrafted couch and chairs with flowered cushions and embroidered pillows stood on the south side and, although the original counter continued to stand between the kitchen and the living area, it had been painted and was now a shiny white. The room looked downright homey.

"Cory," the man called. "We have company."

A buxom, fiftyish-looking woman with a rounded face and yellow-gray hair pulled back into a bun strode around the counter. She took one look at Katherine and Hannah and reached out to them.

"Hey, it's great to see you. We don't get much company out here, especially ladies."

"My name's Katherine and this is my daughter Hannah," Katherine said. "We came looking for my little girl. She was kidnapped a little while ago and . . ."

Cory Bannister stepped back a pace. Her eyes widened with concern. "Oh, I'm so sorry! What can we do to help?"

Katherine and Hannah took seats on the couch and told the story of Faith Ann's disappearance one more time.

"And that's why we have to get to Paradise Lake," Katherine concluded.

"I knew there was something wrong," Hannah blurted. "I just knew it. Maggie was talking about going up to her folks' place just before she took Faith Ann and disappeared."

"Maggie?" Neal arched one eyebrow and searched Katherine's eyes. "There was a Maggie came by here, and she had a little girl with her. They were on their way to her folks' farm."

Katherine's heart pounded in her chest. "That's her. What was the little girl's name?"

"Faith . . . Annie Faith or Faith Anna, or something like that."

"Faith Ann!"

"Yes, Faith Ann."

"That's my baby! I gotta get up there. I gotta get my baby."

"The little girl didn't seem scared or anything," Cory said.

"They were friends," Katherine responded. "And they'd been talking about visiting Maggie's parents."

Hannah's eyes filled with tears, but she didn't speak.

"We'll work something out," Neal said. "We'll find a way." Katherine and Hannah sat for some time with Cory and Neal, talking of babies and loneliness and the pain that losing a child can cause.

"I've got to get to Paradise Lake," Katherine said at last. "There's got to be a way."

Cory leaned forward, her face intent. "You know, I've been puzzling over this thing all this while, and I have a thought. The Ojibwa trail goes straight to Paradise Lake just about seven miles to the east. You could follow it, and it'd take you right up there. The only thing is you'd need a horse or a mule or something."

"Why couldn't we walk?"

"It's a good sixty miles, some of it over rough terrain, that's why," Neal said. "I think you'd have a lot of trouble making it all the way."

"If there's a way up there, I'm going. Please don't try to stop me. I've got to find my baby."

Cory turned to Neal. "We could give them food for the trip, and they wouldn't need to hurry. It'd be better than just sitting here doing nothing."

"Cory," Neal said, "that's an awfully long walk for two women, and I can't go with them with this bum leg. I'd never make it the first five miles."

"Well, there's Meyers' cabin about two-thirds of the way. They could rest there for several days. And like I said, we could give them food and stuff."

Neal raised one eyebrow in a slant. "You aren't really considering this thing, are you?"

Every muscle in Katherine's body tensed. Was there a chance? Could she and Hannah make it to Paradise Lake by themselves?

"Mr. Bannister, we've got to try."

She looked at Hannah and found an almost desperate plea written across the girl's face.

"We've got to do it, Katherine," the young girl said. "We can't just quit, not if there's a chance of finding Faith Ann. We've got to go."

"Well then, let's get started," Cory said. "We'll give you sandwiches for tomorrow and the next day. I'll boil some eggs. They'll keep fairly well for a while. After that, you'll need something more compact—dried beef, maybe a little smoked fish, dried fruits and vegetables."

Cory threw herself into the project like she'd been shot out of a cannon. "And I'll pack some of these snicker-doodles."

She disappeared behind the wall that separated the sleeping quarters from the rest of the building, emerging directly with an old flour sack. She ran a rope around its top to form a drawstring and then packed it with dried meat, dried apples, and other items that were easy to carry.

"In the morning I'll make sandwiches."

Neal exited the building as Cory continued to fulfill her mission. "It'll be cold nights," she said, "so you'll need warm clothing."

She rummaged around and found two pairs of Neal's old overalls, which she cut off just above Katherine and Hannah's ankles. She pulled out some long stockings and two pairs of moccasins she'd gotten in trade from a local Indian. Cory was sure they'd be better for walking than leather shoes.

Soon Neal returned to the shanty with a canteen. "I found this in the old office," he said. "We'll fill it with water just before you leave, and you'll have something to keep you refreshed."

All afternoon, the three women prepared for the long trip. Then, as evening twilight faded, Cory showed Katherine and Hannah to a little-used back room where they might spend the night.

"Hannah can use the top bunk," Cory said, "and Katherine, you can use the bottom."

Minutes later, Katherine crawled into bed. But though she was exhausted, she couldn't sleep. Her mind kept drifting northward to a little place called Paradise Lake.

The next morning Katherine and Hannah packed their dresses in Aunt Mae's suitcase and donned Neal's overalls. They pulled on a couple of Cory's old shirts and stepped into the moccasins she'd given them.

Hannah began to laugh, preening around the room like a fashion model. "Do you think I look all right for the queen's ball?"

Katherine fell onto the bed and joined in the laughter. "We look like a couple of ragamuffins," she responded. "That's what we look like . . . but we'll be warm."

After breakfast, Katherine and Hannah climbed into Neal Bannister's boat, Neal pushed off, and Katherine and Hannah were on their way upriver.

"Be sure to check back when you come this way," Cory called.

"We will," Katherine responded. "And thanks for everything." A thrill of hope glissaded up Katherine's spine. She and Hannah were on the last part of their journey. Although it would be difficult, she knew for sure that Maggie and Faith Ann had come this way. And she meant to find her baby.

It was a short trip upriver, and before long Neal ran his boat ashore. He climbed out of the craft and helped Katherine and Hannah onto the bank.

"Are you sure you want to do this thing?" he asked. "It's a long trip for a strong man."

"We're very sure," Katherine and Hannah responded, almost in chorus. "We have to find Faith Ann."

"Then take my pocket knife and some matches."

Neal reached into his pocket and pulled out a small bag. "You'll find Meyers' cabin to the left of the trail about two-thirds of the way. You can rest there and get a fresh supply of water from the spring. There might even be some food in the place."

Katherine looked out on a wall of giant softwood trees that arched over a corridor through the forest. It was a pathway of hope, and Katherine was determined to make it a roadway to success.

She and Hannah said their goodbyes and started up the Ojibwa trail.

As Katherine walked, she thought about the man she had married and the life they'd planned together. She thought about the happiness they'd known, and her heart was pricked with his loss and what might have been. But at the same time, she felt a degree of warmth in his memory.

I'll find your little one, Frank. I'm almost there.

All morning, Katherine and Hannah tramped over ridges, through valleys, and around marshes. Katherine lugged Aunt Mae's case while Hannah carried Cory's lunch sack, first in one hand and then the other.

By noon, Katherine felt so tired she wanted to collapse in her tracks.

"How' you doing, Hannah," she said at last.

"A little tired, but I'll make it."

"Well, let's find a place to eat; I'm exhausted."

Looking around, Katherine saw a fallen tree with roots exposed and leafage wilted and dying. "How about that tree trunk over there?"

Hannah seemed more than willing to rest.

Katherine took a seat, allowing her body to go as limp as possible and yet remain upright. She let out a long, slow breath. "It sure feels good to sit down."

Hannah opened the lunch Cory had prepared, handed a fish sandwich to Katherine, and took a seat on the tree stock.

Katherine took a bite and almost swooned. "Mmmm, this is the best sandwich I've ever eaten. I didn't realize I was so fond of fish."

Hannah didn't answer. She just closed her eyes and let her body relax.

Soon the sandwiches were gone and the ladies shared several of Cory's snickerdoodles. They drank from the canteen, rested briefly, and went on their way, pressed into action by the urgency of their mission.

Katherine and Hannah walked steadily northward, each consumed by her own introspection. Finally Hannah's thoughts burst forth.

"Why?" she said. "Why didn't I watch? I knew something was wrong, and I didn't watch."

Katherine's heart broke. "Oh, Hannah," she lamented, "don't punish yourself. You weren't to blame."

"But I could feel that something was wrong, and I slept right through it."

"It's OK. You gave us the clue to their whereabouts, and we're going to find them."

"Well, yes. At least I did that right."

"Just leave it with Christ, Hannah, like I did. Then you don't have to worry about it."

In time, the sun faded, evening came, and they found a grassy place for the night. Katherine set Aunt Mae's case upright on the ground to use as a table and laid out some of the eggs Cory had sent. She retrieved some dried apple slices and cookies, and the two women dined in silence, too tired to talk after an exhausting day. It was obvious this walk was going to be one long grueling task.

With supper finished, they lay down on a knoll, fully dressed and with their coats on. Despite the primitive surroundings and a chill in the air, Katherine fell asleep almost immediately.

It was just before daybreak when Katherine awoke to a strange presence in camp. She lay still—afraid to move. And then she saw him.

A man came near, silent as the night. He stood tall and menacing—an Indian in buckskins and moccasins, with a knife in his belt and a tomahawk at his side.

Slowly, stealthily, the Indian opened the flour sack and examined its contents.

Please, God, Katherine prayed, *don't let him take what little supplies we have.* She watched as the man checked the contents of Aunt Mae's case and shook the canteen.

He probed everything in camp and then slipped away into the night without taking a thing.

Katherine lay rigid with terror. As the new day dawned, she and Hannah made a quick exit without breakfast.

All that day the sun shone brightly, filtering through the trees in flecks and speckles. Squirrels churred and birds twittered, but Katherine couldn't forget the image of that early-morning visitor. A world that should have been peaceful brought only anxiety. Exhausted as they were, Katherine and Hannah kept a steady pace all day.

As night fell, they found a dry hollow near a rippling creek where they ate the last two sandwiches and some dried apples.

They filled the canteen with fresh water and lay on the sand, listening to the stream as it babbled and gurgled its way to some distant world. Katherine drifted into slumber but didn't rest well. Again and again she woke with that ominous feeling of an uninvited presence. Again and again she sat up, looked around, and fell back, dozing restlessly. About four in the morning she opened her eyes to see the intruder disappear among the trees.

What did he want? Why was he out there? Shaking off the questions for which she had no answers, Katherine rose and prepared for another day of walking. She walked with her daughter until she thought her legs would surely fall off.

It was late afternoon when Hannah caught sight of Meyers' cabin.

"Hey, look," she cried. "Is that it?"

Katherine peered forward down the trail to see a small log building with tiny windows and a door that looked out on the Ojibwa trail.

"Looks like it might be," she responded.

Hannah hurried ahead, opened the door, and pushed her way inside. Katherine continued to plod along. Her tired bones refused to move any faster.

Hannah came running back to where Katherine trudged along, her face lit up like the morning sun.

"That's it," she cried. "And it's got bunks and blankets and everything—even a little stove for heat."

Katherine almost broke into tears. They just might stay a day or two, long enough to build strength for the remainder of the journey. She smiled as she considered the prospect of sleeping on a real bed.

Entering the cabin, Katherine flopped on the nearest bunk and promptly fell asleep. If the Indian came that night, she didn't know about it.

The next morning, Katherine checked the cupboards and found a box of stale crackers and a single jar of pickles, but no substantial stock. Thank goodness, Cory had packed plenty of food. She and Hannah rested all day and night before returning to their walk.

"God, help us today," Katherine prayed as they left the cabin. "Go with us and help us to complete our mission."

But they'd hardly left the cabin when the sky grew overcast and a drenching rain poured from the heavens. The ground was soaked and there were puddles everywhere. Katherine and Hannah slogged over the squishy ground, watching their step lest they slip and fall in the slimy layer of mud that covered the trail.

Water dripped from Katherine's hair, her eyelashes, her chin. "Lord, I don't understand," she prayed. "You said you'd help and this doesn't seem very helpful at all."

And then it happened. Lightning flashed, thunder boomed, and the forest was filled with the wrenching sound of cracking wood. A great elm tree came crashing down right over the place where Hannah walked.

"Hannah, look out!" Katherine screamed.

Hannah leaped for her life, but she wasn't fast enough. She lay under the tree, unmoving with tree branches holding her fast.

"Hannah!" Katherine fell onto the muddy earth, pulling and yanking at the branches. "Hannah, get up. I can't go on without you. Hannah!"

But Hannah didn't move. She lay silent as a stone.

"Lord, I don't understand," Katherine repeated. "I committed my life to you. You said you'd take care of me. Now Hannah's hurt, I'm alone, and there's no one to help." Heart-rending sobs broke from Katherine's chest.

Suddenly, without a murmur, the big Indian stepped out of the forest, whipped out his tomahawk, and hacked the branches away from Hannah's body.

"Come," he said.

He threw the sack of supplies over his shoulder, swept Hannah into his arms, and took off through the forest.

Katherine grabbed Aunt Mae's case, following with every ounce of strength in her body. Where was he going? She mustn't let him leave her here in the woods.

"Wait," she called. "I can't keep up. Wait." The Indian stopped. "Come," he said.

That night Katherine slept in a wigwam along with the Indian and his squaw. Hannah lay in the medicine shelter with an old woman who watched over her with herbs and potions.

CHAPTER TWENTY-FOUR

Clive Isaman, you old dog," Neal Bannister said as Clive approached. "It's good to see you. What're you doin' up here in God's country?"

Clive wasted no time but got right down to business. "Neal, I'm looking for a couple of women. They should have come through a few days ago. Names are Katherine and Hannah McLean. Have you seen them?"

Neal jammed the shovel he was carrying into the dirt and reached out his hand. "Yes, as a matter of fact I have. They came through a few days ago. They were looking for a little girl by the name of Faith Ann."

"Those are the ones!"

Clive grabbed Neil's hand in both of his own and shook it until it should have fallen off. "You got any idea where they are now?" "Somewhere between here and Paradise Lake, I suppose. They were pretty determined to go, so we gave 'em supplies and took 'em upriver to the Ojibwa Trail."

"Did they seem OK? Do you think they'll make the trip without a problem?"

"The route is pretty clear, they had plenty of supplies, and Meyers' cabin is about two-thirds of the way. It'll be a hard trip, but if they stay on the path and don't try to go too fast, they'll be OK."

"Well, then, if you've got a bed, I'll stay the night and chase them down tomorrow."

"Sure thing. Now c'mon inside and have a bite before you turn in."

Clive stayed the night with the Bannisters and left the next morning, heading upriver with Neal in his boat. Rain pelted them all the way, chilling their bones and soaking their clothes, yet Clive whistled as he went. Katherine was just ahead, and he'd find her soon. He hadn't realized during all those months how important she'd become to him.

At the Ojibwa trail, Clive thanked his host, hopped out of the boat, and hurried up the path with the rapid step of a lumber camp walker. He arrived at Meyers' cabin about noon the next day, stopped for lunch, rested briefly, and continued on his way. Katherine must be just ahead.

And then he saw it—a giant elm lying across the trail. It was obviously a recent fall, for its leaves were still budding and green. Katherine had either passed before it fell or slogged around it. Clive hoped, for her sake, that she hadn't had to do the latter.

He hoisted his backpack, stepped into the muddy duff, and made his way around the fallen tree. Back on the trail he set a brisk pace, hoping to reach Paradise Lake by the next day.

Late in the afternoon after another long day, Clive found himself on the shore at Paradise Lake. The rain had let up and the sky smiled in beautiful azure blue. Not far away stood a cluster of farm buildings, probably Maggie Nilsson's childhood home. Katherine would be there, safe and sound, planning a trip back to Hitchcock with Faith Ann. He walked up to the cottage door and knocked.

Hannah woke to a world of semidarkness. Her head throbbed and her left arm screamed objection every time she moved it. She looked up at walls supported on tall poles and tied together, forming a cone shape above her head. A fire smoldered in a stone pit in the center of the shelter, and two women on the other side of the room mumbled in unintelligible whispers.

Where was she? What was she doing here? And where was Katherine?

One of the women, not much older than Hannah, moved closer. "Good morning," she said in perfect English.

She brushed her hand over her beaded cotton tunic, smoothing it over a long buckskin skirt. "My name is Weonuk. I went to English school for two years, and I speak your language. I'll be here to talk to you and to help you talk to Koyake, the medicine woman."

Hannah looked into a set of dark, caring eyes. "What happened? Where am I? How did I get here?"

"You are in the village of the Great Chief Muktemoko. A tree fell on you, and you have been very sick. My father, Matsowin, brought you to our village. This is the wigwam of Koyake, the medicine woman."

Hannah tried to sit up, and the world grew fuzzy. She dropped back onto the mat where she lay with her head spinning. "Where's my stepmother?"

"Your mother is with my parents. Would you like to see her?"

Hannah nodded. "Yes, please." Maybe Katherine could tell her what was going on.

"You wait. I will get her."

Weonuk left, and the old medicine woman shuffled across the room to Hannah's side.

When Hannah looked up at the woman, her heart almost jumped out of her chest. Pinned to the old woman's blouse was Grandma Hamlin's brooch, its black opal held fast by the golden whorls that Hannah knew so well.

Hannah pointed at the brooch. "Pretty pin."

The old woman smiled and mumbled something that sounded like, "Anzenagong." She patted Hannah's shoulder. "Anzenagong." She stood in the murky light for many long minutes, leaning over the bed, straightening the covers and patting the pillow.

Hannah's heart throbbed. It was her brooch, she was sure of it. The old woman smiled, turned, and padded across the room. In time, Weonuk returned with Katherine. "Are you still awake? I've brought your mother."

Katherine came near, and Weonuk moved to the other side of the wigwam to visit with the medicine woman.

"You 'bout scared the wits out of me," Katherine said. "If it hadn't been for Matsowin, I don't know what I'd have done—out there in the woods with you lying unconscious under a tree, and no place to go and no one to help."

Hannah motioned with her hand and Katherine leaned close. "Go take a look at that old woman's chest," she whispered. "She's wearing Grandma Hamlin's brooch."

"What? Are you sure? How would she get Grandma Hamlin's brooch?"

"I don't know, but she's got it. If we can get our hands on it for a minute, we'll find my initials on the back."

"I'll try to get a look at it when I leave. For now, you just wait. If it really is your brooch, it'll be OK for the time being."

Just then, Koyake shuffled over from the other side of the room. Katherine observed the brooch on her chest and shot a glance of recognition in Hannah's direction.

Koyake busied herself in close proximity, stepping between Hannah and Katherine, silently asserting her authority.

Finally, the old woman wandered across the teepee, returning with a tin cup full of some awful-smelling brown liquid.

"Embat," the woman said. "Embat, embat." She held the cup to Hannah's lips, and Hannah gulped the stuff, shivering with the acrid taste.

The medicine woman walked away, and almost immediately Hannah found herself strolling through a beautiful garden. She saw morning glories and irises and roses. She saw wildflowers—daisies and daffodils and buttercups. As Hannah walked, a voice called out to her: *All this beauty belongs to you. Choose what you want. Hannah reached out and picked one beautiful, ruby red rose.* She pinned the rose to her dress, smiling with satisfaction.

Then, somehow it was all gone, and Hannah was slogging through a dark, muddy swamp. Black slime clung to her legs and thorns stabbed at her arms. "Help," she called. Somebody help me." She reached out for a hand and nearly fell off the pallet. Opening her eyes, she stared into the blackness of night.

Hannah lay trembling in the darkness, waiting for early morning light.

"Weonuk," Hannah said, when the Indian maiden came to visit. "The medicine woman wears a very pretty pin. Can you tell me where she got it?"

Weonuk smiled. "A little while ago a woman named Maggie came through the village with her daughter."

Maggie! Hannah's muscles tensed at the sound of the name. Was it possible? Could it be?

"The woman was very ill, and my father took her across the fields to the midwife-doctor for help. After they left, Koyake found the pin in the dirt."

"Weonuk," Hannah said, her heart pounding with excitement, "the pin is mine. It came from my Grandmother Hamlin. It has her initials on the back, and my initials are right underneath."

Weonuk's brow furrowed. "That is very strange. Are you sure?"

"The little girl is my sister, Faith Ann. And the woman, Maggie, stole her in the middle of the night. Please, Weonuk, go tell my stepmother to come here right away."

After Weonuk left, Hannah lay still, pondering the events that had brought her to this place.

The minutes dragged like hours, until at last Katherine entered the tent. "C'mere." Hannah's lips barely spoke the words.

Katherine's eyes widened as Hannah shared the information Weonuk had given.

"If that's true," she said, "then we've found Faith Ann. Takemos can take us right to her."

"It's true, Katherine. I know it is. We've got to get out of here." Then and there, Katherine and Hannah made plans to leave the village. "But first, let's talk to Weonuk about the brooch."

Two days later, after conferring with Weonuk and Koyake, and with the chief's permission, Hannah tucked Grandmother Hamlin's brooch into Aunt Mae's suitcase and prepared to leave.

Looking back, she could see Weonuk and Koyake standing at a distance waving goodbye. Koyake wore a smile that spread from ear to ear as she raised her hand to her throat, fingering the lace collar of Katherine's blue poplin dress.

Then, with her left arm in a sling and feeling a bit dizzy, Hannah turned to accompany Katherine and Takemos out of camp.

Clive shifted back and forth on his feet, waiting for Maggie's folks to come to the door. Where were these people? Why didn't they answer? He knocked again and stood waiting in the stillness. Why was he so nervous? He was almost as ill at ease as he'd been that night so long ago when he'd held Katherine close and kissed her for the first time.

He tapped his feet and stood jingling the change in his pocket. Finally, he gave up and descended the steps, heading down the path toward an old unpainted barn that stood behind the house.

A newly plowed piece of ground, probably a garden plot, lay on his right, and a corn crib and chicken coop on his left. As Clive passed the chicken coop, a woman stepped out of the door carrying a bucket.

"Hello, I'm Clive Isaman and I'm looking for the Parishes. Is this their place?"

The old woman brushed her free hand across her thinning white hair and stepped back, regarding Clive with interest. "This here's the Parish farm, all right. What do you want?"

"I'm looking for a couple of women who came this way. One is named Katherine McLean, and the other is her stepdaughter, Hannah. Have you seen them?"

"Never heard of them."

"Well, what about a woman named Maggie Nilsson? Do you know anything about her?"

"Yes. Maggie's my daughter, but if you're looking for her, you're out of luck. She left here years ago, right after she married that Nilsson fella."

Clive's heart dove into his shoes. If Maggie hadn't come here, where had she gone? And where was Katherine?

"I knew Maggie down-state," he explained. "Recently she lost her daughter, and it hit her pretty hard. She said something about coming up here."

"Well, we haven't seen her or hardly even heard from her since she left the place fifteen years ago."

Clive paused, considering his options. "After her daughter died, Maggie was so depressed she walked away in the middle of the night . . . with my friend's little girl."

Pain and horror cascaded across Mrs. Parish's face. "Are you sure? I don't believe Maggie would do such a thing."

"I guess I wouldn't have thought so, either. But she was pretty distraught. The man down at Hopewell said Maggie had been there and she was headed this way."

"Well, Maggie knows how to survive in the woods, and I think she'll take good care of the little girl, so you don't need to worry about that. Just a minute, I'll call George, and we'll see what we can do. The name's Gretchen, Gretchen Parish."

Gretchen turned, put down the bucket, and lifted her hands to her mouth to let out a piercing wail. "George is out picking up rocks in the west field," she said. "He'll come when he hears my call."

Clive and Gretchen went inside and Gretchen started a pot of coffee.

Soon, George Parish pushed open the door. He pulled off his red-plaid jacket and hung it on a nail.

"What's up, Gretchen?"

"George, this man says Maggie ran off with someone's little girl. They thought she might be coming here."

George's eyebrows knit in consternation. "That doesn't seem like our Maggie."

Once again, Clive went over the events of Faith Ann's disappearance, while George Parish sat listening and shaking his head in disbelief.

"Well," George said at last, "I reckon your best bet is to ask at church on Sunday. If Maggie's in the area, someone will know."

Clive agreed to stay with the Parishes until Sunday, and though he spent entire days walking from farm to farm seeking the women, his search brought no results. He went to church on Sunday, and the preacher made an announcement regarding the loss, but no one seemed to have any information.

"Let us pray for this lost child," the preacher said. And the people's prayers were offered up to heaven.

Clive left the church with a heavy heart. Where were Maggie and Faith Ann? Where were Katherine and Hannah? Why hadn't any of them arrived at Paradise Lake?

As he walked toward his host's carriage, Clive heard a highpitched cry. "Hey mister."

He turned to find a barefoot little girl running after him. "Hey, mister, wait a minute. I got something to tell you."

The little girl came closer, looking up at Clive from a face smudged with dirt and framed in scraggly, red hair.

Clive regarded the child critically. What could this ragged little kid do for him? "What's your name, young lady?"

"I'm Helen Shank, and there's a little girl out at the midwife's house. Her ma's real sick and they're stayin' there 'til she gets better."

"So where does this midwife live?"

"She lives across the Muktewak Swamp. My pa takes me there sometimes when he goes to fix stuff. And the lady that lives there gives us pies 'n' things for the work."

"Are your ma and pa here, so I could talk to them?"

"No, my ma's dead and my pa works awful hard, so he's tired on Sunday."

"If I go to your house, can I talk to your pa?"

"Yes. He'll be up by now, and you can talk as much as you want."

"Well, wait a minute, while I tell my friends where I'm going, and then I'll walk you home."

Clive took a moment to tell Gretchen and George what he'd learned and then reached out for Helen Shank's hand. "OK, let's go see your pa."

"I think this may be the girl you're looking for," Helen's pa said, when Clive explained his mission. "She's a girl about four years old with short, brown, curly hair—kind of like yours, actually. She seems quite smart."

Clive's heart began to thump inside his chest. Had he found Faith Ann? What about Katherine? Where was Katherine and why was she not here at the Parishes?

CHAPTER TWENTY-FIVE

Katherine and Hannah stood at the edge of the Muktewak swamp, looking west at a large, two-story, stone house with a long lane leading up to it from the south. The swamp bordered it on the east and north, and a row of low, forested hills rose behind it on the west. An old pump stood in the yard with a large willow tree nearby. One thought resonated in Katherine's mind. Her baby might be waiting within those walls.

"Thank you, Takemos," she said. "I really appreciate . . ."

But Takemos stood silent—straight and tall, unapproachable. "Go," he said.

Katherine took a deep breath and headed toward the building. "Goodbye, Takemos," she called. "Goodbye, and thanks for everything."

The only response was the gentle whisper of a spring breeze. Takemos had disappeared into the swamp.

Katherine hurried across the field, filled with fresh hope that Faith Ann might soon be in her arms. With each step, her excitement grew and, without realizing it, she quickened her pace until she was almost running. Hannah ran two steps ahead.

As Katherine drew near the building, she noticed a woman standing in the yard with her back turned, hanging a sheet on the line to dry.

"Hello," Katherine called.

The woman clipped a clothespin over the sheet and turned to walk across the yard toward Katherine and Hannah.

"Hello," she called. "What can I do for you?"

"I . . . uh I . . . we I . . ." Butterflies fluttered in Katherine's stomach. "An Indian named Takemos brought us here," she stammered.

"Yes, I know Takemos. He's a fine man, and I've appreciated his support."

"He said he left a sick woman in your care not long ago."

"Yes, that's true; he does that from time to time. I'm Joy Barker and this is my midwifery."

Katherine's heart thumped in her chest. "He said there was a little girl with her."

"Right again. But what do you want with them?"

Just then, the door flew open and Faith Ann appeared. "Mama!" she cried.

Bounding across the porch and down the steps, she threw herself into Katherine's arms, clinging with a grasp of steel.

Relief flooded Katherine's being, and she broke into tears of joy.

"My baby, my baby!" she cried. "Hannah, we've found our baby."

Katherine opened her arms, and Hannah threw herself into the embrace. Together the family wept great tears of relief.

Katherine relaxed her grip and turned to Joy Barker.

"Faith Ann is my daughter," she said. "The woman who brought her here was a neighbor down-state, and she took Faith Ann in the middle of the night."

Dismay washed over Joy Barker's face. "But Maggie seemed like such a nice person. I can't imagine I . . ."

"Maggie was a fine woman. She just lost her balance when her daughter died."

Faith Ann continued to cling, so Katherine pulled the child close once more and moved toward the porch. She took a seat on the steps, where she sat for many long minutes, soothing the whimpering child.

In time, Faith Ann looked up at her mother. "Mama, Mrs. Maggie got real sick, and Miss Joy tried to help her, but she couldn't."

"I know, sweetheart. I know."

"Then Mrs. Maggie went to be with Jesus, and I got scared 'cause I was alone, and I didn't know anybody."

Katherine's heart went out to her little girl, so trusting and still fond of Maggie. She could see no point in disrupting that esteem, so she just pulled the child close and kissed her on the cheek.

Faith Ann wiped at her eyes. "Miss Joy said I could stay with her 'til you could come and get me. An' I waited and waited like a big girl, but you didn't come and sometimes I cried."

"You were a big girl," Katherine said. "Sometimes even big girls cry."

"Well, let's go inside," Joy Barker said, "and I'll fill you in on the events of the last week or so."

Inside, Katherine and Hannah sat with Joy Barker as the woman told her story.

"Takemos brought Maggie and Faith Ann here," she said, "because Maggie was ill, and the tribe didn't want the white woman to die in their village. I did all I could for her, but she passed away of the fever several days after she and Faith Ann arrived. We buried her behind the house at the foot of Muktewak Hill. I didn't know how to contact next of kin or where to go for information about Faith Ann, so we just waited. All she could tell me was that her mama and sister were in a lumber camp and that Uncle Ned and Aunt Mae were out there somewhere."

Pain overspread Katherine's spirit. "And we had no idea where to look."

Hannah leaned in. "But I finally figured out where they went," she said. "I was looking at pictures in my bedroom, when I remembered Maggie said she'd like to go to her folks' place at Paradise Lake."

Hannah smiled, as she hadn't since Faith Ann's disappearance. "And Faith Ann wanted to go swimming there."

"Yes, but how did you manage to end up here? Paradise Lake is some distance north."

Katherine's heart grew tender, remembering her prayer in the woods.

You said you'd take care of me. Now Hannah's hurt, I'm alone and there's no one to help.

"I believe it was the hand of God," she said. "I asked Him to help and He sent Takemos to watch over us before we even knew we needed him."

Katherine went over the story of Koyake and the brooch, and all the while Faith Ann sat with arms clinging tightly to her mother.

"Well, it sounds like divine intervention to me," Joy Barker said. "So, what are your plans now?"

"I really hadn't thought about that," Katherine responded. "The only thing on my mind has been the search for Faith Ann." She gave her daughter a little squeeze. "I suppose we'll need to find a way back to Hopewell and then take the train to Hitchcock."

"Then I suggest you contact Hans Oberman. He has a small wagon and he might be able to take you to Hopewell sometime soon."

The next afternoon, Katherine and her girls walked with Joy Barker to Hans Oberman's farm. The sun shone brightly in a beautiful azure sky, creating a perfect backdrop for the delight that filled Katherine's breast. Her heart soared as she walked hand in hand with her daughter down a dusty, two-track, road.

"Good morning, Joy," Mrs. Oberman said, as she opened the door. "What a surprise!"

"Verna, we've found Faith Ann's mother."

Joy nudged Katherine forward. "This is Katherine McLean and her other daughter, Hannah. Takemos brought them through the swamp yesterday afternoon."

Verna Oberman swung the door wide, motioning for the women's entry. "Well thank goodness. We've been hunting all over the county trying to find you ladies."

Katherine and the girls followed Joy into the house, where Katherine went over the story of Faith Ann's disappearance.

"And we were wondering if Hans might have time to take them back to Hopewell," Joy said.

"I wouldn't be the least surprised," Verna responded. "He's been concerned about Faith Ann, too."

When Hans came for dinner, Verna suggested a trip to Hopewell. "We'll make a way," he said. "We've been really worried about that little girl."

Hans paused, apparently considering his options. "We can leave early Thursday morning," he said at last.

Katherine spent the next several days working about the place with Joy. They baked bread, churned butter, and cleaned lamp chimneys. They fed chickens, gathered eggs, and mended socks. And one day she and the girls went up the hillside with Joy to gather morels. There was no treat like those mushrooms in spring. Her heart sang with high hope that her world had finally come together and she could keep her promise to Frank. Soon, she and her daughters would build a life in Hitchcock.

It was late in the afternoon after a busy day when Katherine sat on the porch visiting with Joy. Hannah and Faith Ann played nearby with Barney, Joy's mongrel dog. Hannah brushed her hand across Barney's side and he rolled over, allowing the girls to rub his tummy. Faith Ann snuggled close, and the dog licked her face. She rolled away, brushing her cheek with her hand.

"Mama," she said, "Barney kisses just like Sabaka." "Yes," Katherine responded. "Barney loves you, too."

She relaxed, letting her eyes wander along the line of trees that bordered the swamp. It was then that she spotted someone moving across the field.

"Look, Joy," she said, pointing. It was a man and he carried a pack on his back.

"Probably Takemos," Joy responded. "Or maybe Bert Schank; he comes around every now and then to do odd jobs around the place, and in return I give him baked goods and things."

But Faith Ann was not confused. "Mama, it's Mr. Clive!"

The little girl bolted across the yard toward the figure, with Hannah close behind.

Looking more closely, Katherine could see that Faith Ann was right; it was Clive.

How do you suppose he comes to be out here? Katherine couldn't believe how good she felt to see him.

Coming closer, Clive swept Faith Ann into his arms, whirling around, laughing and hugging the little girl who, unbeknown to him, was his daughter. Hannah drew near, and he put Faith Ann down to greet the young woman. Then the three of them walked hand in hand across the field toward the house.

Suddenly Katherine became aware of a longing she hadn't realized existed.

"Clive, what are you doing out here?" she called as he drew near.

"Looking for you," Clive responded.

He spoke of his visit in Hitchcock and his concern for Katherine's safety. "So I came along in case you needed help."

Katherine smiled to think he cared enough to go to all that trouble.

The remainder of the day was filled with talk of walking in the woods and of Indians and of a desperate search for one little girl. "When that tree fell on Hannah," Katherine said. "I thought that would be the end of both of us."

Clive picked up the story. "And that's where I missed you. I came upon that tree right after the rain and assumed you had passed before it fell."

In time, evening came, Faith Ann was tucked into bed, and Katherine and Clive wandered outside. There they stood near the willow tree, looking up at the night sky with its panorama of starlit serenity.

"This is really a beautiful place," Katherine murmured. "So quiet and peaceful."

"Yes it is," Clive agreed. "Makes you want to settle down right here and build a family."

Katherine's heart fluttered in her chest.

"Katherine," Clive said softly, "I never realized how important you are to me. It nearly broke my heart when I arrived in Hitchcock and you were gone. I've been racing through the woods, hoping against hope that you were OK and that I could see you again."

"I'm glad you came. It was a long, hard trip. Sometimes I thought I just couldn't go on. But I had to find my baby."

They talked long and earnestly of recent days and of lifelong purpose.

Clive slipped his arm around Katherine's waist. "Katherine," he said, "do you think you could ever love me again?"

Katherine's breath caught in her throat. "Clive, I have something to tell you. I've given my heart to Jesus, and I need someone who shares my conviction."

Moonlight revealed surprise on Clive's face, but it quickly melted into tenderness.

"Katherine." Clive stepped back, looking intently into Katherine's eyes. "Luc led me to the Lord two winters ago, and news that you've accepted Him, too, is the best thing I could think of for a wife."

A wife! Katherine's heart leaped in her chest. Was this a proposal of marriage? If so, there was a certain matter she needed to clear up first.

"Clive there's something else that I've been keeping from you, and when you hear it you may not want to be my husband."

"I can't imagine anything that would change my feelings for you."

Katherine hesitated, took a deep breath and rushed forward. "I've been lying to you. Faith Ann is not Frank's child. She's your daughter, conceived on that last night before you went away. I've kept it from you all this time."

Clive gazed at Katherine in stunned silence.

Was he angry? Would he walk out of her life forever? Tears welled in her eyes as she waited, fearing he'd leave, and she'd be alone again as she was so many years ago.

Then slowly, gently, he brushed his thumbs across her cheeks and pulled her close in a heartfelt embrace. The kiss they shared told it all. Their youthful love was gone, and in its place had grown a strong bond, worthy of matrimony.

"Katherine," Clive whispered. "I've always felt a special bond with Faith Ann, and I want to be her pa. Please say you'll marry me."

A surge of contentment overspread Katherine's soul. "I'll be happy to marry you, Mr. Isaman," she murmured.

The next morning, when Hannah learned of the upcoming marriage, her eyes shone with pleasure. "That's wonderful," she said. "I can't think of anyone who could be a better substitute for my pa."

Clive slipped his arm around Katherine's waist and reached out to his daughters. "And I'll do my best to fulfill that responsibility."

Some months later, Katherine and Clive were married in the little church in Hitchcock. Hannah was radiant, as she preceded her mother down the aisle, and Faith Ann glowed with pride while strewing flowers along the way.

Uncle Ned gave the bride away, and Aunt Mae sat proud and beaming in the mother's pew.

Katherine's dreams had come true at last. She was truly . . . finally . . . home.

EPILOGUE

Traveling the highways and byways along the northern tier of the United States one can see remnants of the great timberland that once covered the area. Though new growth has sprung up, old stumps continue to dot the ground in many places. Moving closer one becomes aware of the immense proportions of these heralds of yesteryear—trees that stood a hundred feet tall—one of which, it is said, might provide lumber for an entire house.

The trees were felled and transported to market by tough men who worked long hours, lived in spare quarters and received little pay. Their day began early in the morning and ended late at night with only Sunday as a day of rest. Axemen notched trunks, sawyers hewed trees, and loaders helped place logs on sleighs. There were swampers to cut off branches, teamsters to manage horses, skidders to help haul logs.

In spring the river drives began. Hundreds of logs that had been stamped with the company's mark and decked beside lakes and rivers were sent hurtling down waterways. Tough men jumped from log to log, breaking up jams and guiding the timber along. Other men followed, becoming soaked in the icy flow as they retrieved "strays" and pushed them back into the waterway.

It was dangerous work. Falling trees or swinging branches could snuff out a man's life in a moment's time. Then the lifeless body might ride home to wives and children on the tote wagon, mangled and frozen. River hogs could fall beneath the logs and be crushed to death or drown and the body lost or unrecognizable.

These men were silent giants of history, living in anonymity while producing wealth for the lumber barons and for our nation as a whole. This was the lumber camp world.

While women were not considered part of the lumber camp culture, there were those who did participate. Probably the earliest participants were cooks who came with husbands as did Emma with Jasper. Some women, like Sister Olivia, came to the camps as missionaries, and these were generally afforded more acceptance and respect than their male counterparts.

Later in time, the camps provided small shacks near the operation where families might come to spend the winter. In those situations the lumber jack husband spent nights and Sundays with his family.

BIBLIOGRAPHY OF SONGS IN THE PUBLIC DOMAIN

"Amazing Grace," John Newton – 1800

"Blessed Assurance," Fanny Crosby – 1873

"Boy Blue," Author Unknown – 1800's

"Jingle Bells," James Lord Pierpont – 1857

"Maggie Murphy's Home," Author Unknown – 1857

"My Bonnie Lies Over the Ocean," Author Unknown – 1800s

"Nearer My God to Thee," Henry Frances Lyte – 1841

"Turkey in the Straw," Author Unknown – 1800s

ABOUT THE AUTHOR

DAWN BATTERBEE MILLER is the author of *God's Family Tree,* published in 1994 by Church Growth Institute, and numerous articles published worldwide in various Christian periodicals. For several years she served as editor and publisher of *Women in Ministry,* a denominational women's paper. She is also a public school teacher and holds master's degrees in education  and communication arts. Dawn is uniquely equipped to write about nineteenth-century lumber camps. Having been raised in deep woods territory, she grew up steeped in family stories and the local lore of the lumberjack.

Available Titles

God's Family Tree, published by Church Growth Inst.

Pioneer Potpourri, published by DocUmeant Publishing

Deep Wood Series, published by DocUmeant Publishing
First published by WinePress Publishing
  Footprints Under the Pines
  Lost in the Deep Woods